Jungle Series

Written By LI DI

I0526964

A story about
courage and responsibility

Horrifying

Forest

Original Title: 《这里是恐怖的森林》

Original book by The Writers Publishing House Co.,Ltd.

This edition is published by arrangement with Prunus Press USA, through the agency of China National Publications Import and Export (Group) Co., Ltd.

All rights reserved.

A HORRIFYING FOREST

Written by Li Di

Translated by Haiwang Yuan

Designed by Brandy Ding

First edition 2022

ISBN: 978-1-61612-148-8

Prunus Press USA

Contents

Chapter 1

A middle-aged Aini[1] man dressed in black homespun cloth shirt and pants waded through the gurgling Lanmang River leading a white horse. Then, he took a winding path traversed by horse caravan merchants and entered the Yuehagu Forest.

In the Aini vernacular, "yuehagu" means "horrifying."

Such a name alone showed how much the inhabitants here scared this endless, primeval forest.

It was a world shrouded in darkness for ages.

Tens of thousands of crowns vied with one another in shielding the sunlight, thus forming a gigantic, opaque umbrella.

The Yuehagu Forest mercilessly punished anyone who dared to venture into it.

---

[1] Aini is a branch of the ethnic Hani, one of the minority ethnic groups in Yunnan Province, China

Subtropical trees grew so densely as if they were people standing hand in hand to form one labyrinth after another. A nyone who entered them would lose their bearings. If someone chose to go forward, then they would not be able to move an inch as they would be blocked by the huge nets woven by intertwining python-thick vines hanging between the trees.

At a moment like this, a leopard panting with its tongue out might suddenly pounce from behind and put its hairy paws with sharp claws on a traveler's shoulders. As soon as he turned his head to look, the big cat would slit his throat with a single bite. When a leopard ate a man, it would tear his stomach open and gobble up his internal organs first. Then, it would drag the remaining body up to a tree and hang it there so that he could return to devour it after sunset the next day. The sight could be truly horrendous.

Even if a person was lucky enough not to run into a leopard, he might suddenly see face to face with a hungry wolf or a prowling bear. A lone wolf is known to be the most ruthless. And, digging its muzzle into the ground, it could howl in a pack of wolves, which would tear the person to pieces. A foraging bear was not to be messed with either. It was able to lick a man's face off, not to speak of whamming him to a pulp with a single strike of its paw.

To escape? There are countless beasts of prey with their eyes glowing in the depths of this primeval forest punctuated with dim blue will-o'-the-wisps. Even the insidious swamps concealed by dried twigs and fallen leaves were ready to devour their victims with their mouths wide open. Even before submerging in the bog, one would fall a victim to a fierce-looking marsh crocodile, which would crawl over wiggling its bumpy body and smashes one's head with its flicking tail.

However, what gave the locals goosebumps at the mere mention of the Yuehagu Forest was not the natural hazards intrinsic to it.

It was the bandits lurking in this beast-infested forest—a band of bandits that killed people without batting an eye.

These beasts in human skin were the real enemies of the innocent locals!

Among these "beasts," there were hardened house robbers, fiendish highwaymen, outrageous rapists, as well as straggling soldiers whose regiments had been disbanded due to lost battles.

Ganging up, they lorded over the forest as despots, robbed travelers on their way, and murdered people for their money.

In addition, they often pillaged nearby ethnic Aini-inhabited villages either at dawn or dusk. They killed people and burned houses while yelling and cursing, torch and sword or gun in other.

Especially recently, as a bandit-suppressing PLA unit was pressing into the frontiers, the bandits escalated their plundering activities in anticipation of their doomsday. The victimized Aini inhabitants turned pale or became jittery at the mere mention of the bandits.

The bandit-infested forest cast a shadow over the hearts of the inhabitants like a dark cloud casting its shadow over the earth.

It seemed that this middle-aged man, leading his white horse into the forest, was going to visit his relatives across the border.

On the horseback there were two rattan baskets filled with food and clothing.

He had removed the nine brass bells from the neck of the horse lest they might alert the bandits. It is customary for the Aini people to have the bells attached to their horses.

He trod on the mountain path leading to the border, with fallen leaves crunching under his bare feet.

At this moment, the primeval forest was eerily quiet. Only the droplets of moisture, condensed due to excessive humidity, kept dripping from the branches and leaves, thereby forming a "forest drizzle" characteristic of the sub-tropical zone.

He was walking and walking when, all of a sudden, the white horse reared up neighing.

The middle-aged man gave a shudder.

Then, whoosh!

A coir rope was instantly dropped from a tall tropical almond tree and lassoed him by the neck.

He reached his hands desperately to grab it.

But it was too late.

The noose was tightened abruptly when the rope was jerked up. The middle-aged man instantly stopped breathing without a whimper.

His body was hanging from the tropical almond tree.

It happened so suddenly that the white horse had no idea what was going on.

Raising its head, it stuck out its tongue and kept licking the mud-stained soles of its owner.

It remembered that every time its owner overslept after a long trip, it could wake him up by licking his soles.

The white horse licked and licked when suddenly it was startled. Neighing, it took flight and sped into the depth of the forest.

A tiger darted out of a thicket and ran after the horse while sticking up its tail.

In a thick forest with entangled branches and twigs, the white horse could not gallop at full speed. Soon, the tiger caught up.

It bucked and kicked trying to keep away from the tiger.

The tiger was not bothered at all.

Dodging the horse's hooves, the tiger ran around to the flank of the horse as if to race it.

But when it got neck and neck with the horse, the tiger suddenly turned its head and caught the horse's neck in its mouth.

The white horse collapsed.

It fell in a pool of blood.

Before it breathed its last breath, it cast a look in the direction where it had parted with its owner.

This was its last look!

It was trying to tell its owner that it had led the tiger away at the cost of its own life.

However, it would never know that its own had given his life up to the Yuehagu Forest.

Dust flew into the forest quietly flapping its grayish wings.

It announced to the forest that darkness and horror would soon befall it.

A forest python with its body marked with a botched pattern slithered forward with its undulating belly scales and wound its way slowly around tree to tree.

It was foraging to tide over the night.

Suddenly, it detected the middle-aged man hanging from the tree.

It was excited.

It sped up crawling.

It climbed up to the tropical almond tree and, perching itself on a mossy crotch, opened its large fierce-looking mouth and pounced on the middle-aged man's cadaver.

A forest python capable of swallowing a whole red deer or siphoning a shoal of fish from a river could devour a motionless human body with the slightest effort.

Before long, its neck began to expand, as if it were pumped up.

Half of the middle-aged man's body together with the coir rope around his neck was already in the forest python's mouth.

The python kept swallowing the rest of the body.

It knew that its stomach could never burst.

With the entire body in its stomach, the python could crush it into a meat pie by wrapping itself around a tree and pressed its belly hard against it.

Then, it would open its big mouth and regurgitated the uncrushable bones...

This middle-aged man eaten by the python was a scout named Big Liu.

Chapter 2

"Five days have passed, but we haven't heard anything from Big Liu."

Gu Ming's tone was solemn.

As a commander of a reconnaissance company, he had been worried and anxious, so much so that his voice became weak and gruff.

He directed his pensive eyes through the propped-open bamboo window into the Yuehagu Forest enshrouded in the twilight.

Flapping their snow-white wings, a flock of little egrets on their way back to perch skimmed across the top of the thickets and disappeared in the distance.

"Maybe Big Liu is in difficulty. Maybe..."

Gu Ming stopped short.

He hated to put his suspicion into words:

"Maybe he'll never be able to return like the previous two scouts."

Gu Ming paused a long time before withdrawing his eyes from the distance.

He turned around and looked at the two men standing behind him up and down with care and concern.

One of them was Mang Lege, a reconnaissance squad leader.

The other was Guo Sha, a newly recruited soldier of the Aini ethnic background.

A typical Aini man, Mang Lege had big eyes, high nose bridge, and thick lips dyed purple by *binlang*.[2] His square face was heavily tanned by the scorching sun.

Gu Ming had gotten to know this man as he led his reconnaissance company into the border region.

That afternoon, the soldiers who had successively surmounted two mountains were blocked by a primeval forest. Gu Ming ordered that everyone rest in place before taking two

[2] *Binlang* sounds exactly like the Chinese term for areca nut, but it is a round-shaped chew that the ethnic Aini people concocted from boiled teak leaves with lime. They chew it for its refreshing effect.

soldiers with him to explore the way.

As they pressed forward by slashing road-blocking vines with their machetes, they tried to figure out where they were going with the help of their military map.

They were treading forward when suddenly a female bear pounced out of a tree hole growling and threw Gu Ming onto the ground. The two soldiers were panicked and caught in a predicament: to shoot the bear, they feared they might hurt Gu Ming, but if not, Gu Ming could be in greater danger.

While they were at a loss what to do, they suddenly heard someone shouting *"Kujie!"*[3]

An Aini man leaped out of the thickets before his shout dissipated.

He squeezed through the two soldiers, plunged himself before the female bear, and leveled his copper blunderbuss.

He thrusted the muzzle at one of the bear's eyes.

The bear tilted its head up and dodged the muzzle.

Taking this opportunity, the Aini man pulled the trigger…

Bang!

His copper blunderbuss fired.

But the projectiles flew into the sky.

Scared out of its wits, the female bear took to its heels and fled into the primeval forest.

---

[3] "Kujie" is a term of the Aini dialect meaning "jump aside"

The Aini man said beaming, "We can't hurt her. She had her cubs to suckle!"

With that, he helped Gu Ming on his feet.

Before they had time to start a conversation, a male bear dashed from the forest.

Gee, from the same family!

Giving the Aini man no chance to evade its attack, it had put its paws on his shoulders.

Casting away his copper blunderbuss, the Aini man pressed his hands on the bear's paws and retracted his neck. Taking advantage of the momentum, he pushed and pinned the bear's lower jaw with the top of his head.

The male bear opened its mouth as wide as it could while snorting ferociously.

It wanted to bite the man but it could not lower its jaw; it wanted to claw the man but it could not pull its paws from the man's hands pressing hard on them.

Anxious and angry, it growled so loud that it shook some leaves off the trees.

After a moment's stalemate, the Aini man bent forward and dragged the bear's paws downward with all his might. Shouting something like "Kiai," he pulled the bear to the front over his back and threw it to the ground rolling.

Picking itself up, the male bear fled into the primeval forest without looking back.

This Aini man who had conquered two bears in a row was Mang Lege.

He was recommended by his fellow villagers to be a guide for the reconnaissance company.

With the PLA's approval, Mang Lege joined the army and became a reconnaissance squad leader.

Guided by him, the reconnaissance company reached the Yuehagu Forest on the border after trekking across mountains and rivers.

On their way, the reconnaissance company recruited a few Aini young men to improve its reconnaissance efficiency. Guo Sha was one of them. This young man of medium build was liked by everyone for his sharpness.

The company encamped at Gehei Village.

Gu Ming set his orderly room in a stilt bamboo house.

He had two neighbors: one was Grandpa Gong Bu, a single hunter in his fifties; and the other, Ba Muli, the paternal uncle of the new soldier Guo Sha.

After settling down, the reconnaissance company began to get information about the bandits to pave the way for their extermination by the coming bandit-suppressing troops.

But neither of the two scouts that he had dispatched had returned. Gu Ming felt extremely anxious.

His worries were twofold: the safety of the scouts and the urgency of the reconnaissance mission.

Now, nothing was heard either about or from Big Liu either. Gu Ming decided to dispatch Mang Lege and Guo Sha to continue their unfinished task. As ethnic Aini locals, they knew their language and the terrain. All things considered, they were the most suitable for the task.

Before their departure, Gu Ming surveyed Mang Lege and Guo Sha with great concern.

He said, "In a few days, the bandit-suppressing troops will arrive at Gehei Village, but we haven't figured out the bandits' pattern of activities yet. We're in the open while they're in the dark. So, our troops would suffer considerable casualties and, of course, fail to accomplish their mission if they went into the forest to suppress the bandits. If the bandits escaped to the other side of the border, they'd become trouble in future. Now gathering, now scattering, they seem to have some communication mechanism. We must find ways to lure them out of the primeval forest so that our troops can wipe them out. So, Mang Lege and Guo Sha, you've got a very important task..."

Gu Ming had barely finished when a boy hopped in through the bamboo window and landed on the floor with a thump.

The boy was not tall, wearing a short shirt, a pair of loose pants, and a red-cloth turban-like headwear. As soon as he stood on his feet, he greeted Gu Ming with a hand salute:

"Sir, I'm here to report! I guarantee to accomplish the mission!"

His appearance enlivened the depressing atmosphere. Gu Ming, Mang Lege, and Guo Sha all blurted out.

"Ge Long!"

Ge Long was the son of Mang Lege,[4] who had just celebrated his thirteenth birthday. He was a lookalike of his father in terms of his features: heavily tanned face with a high nose bridge, thick lips, and a pair of sparkling eyes. Only that he was of a small stature with slender limbs, making him look like a monkey.

However, despite his small build, the boy possessed sheer masculine strength. He could climb a tree to catch birds, dive into the water to hand fish, fire a gun or a blunderbuss, and draw a bow to shoot. He dared to walk in the dark, go deep into dense woods, venture into the primeval forest, and hunt for wild animals—there was almost nothing he dared not do. A good student of his father, Mang Lege, he was particularly good at archery and tree climbing.

One day, without his father's knowledge, he went into the primeval forest with his bows and arrows. As he ventured deeper and deeper, he ran into a wild buffalo. It weighed more than four hundred kilograms and had wrinkled skin that was nearly bullet-proof. A wild buffalo was not to be messed with! Ge Long, however, did not care. He drew his bow and sent an arrow flying. It hit straight and true on the nose of the buffalo, which instantly flew into a rage and let out a blaring moo of wrath. Ge Long was so scared that he took flight, but the beast was hot on his heels with its horns aiming at his back. It was about to catch up when Mang Lege

---

[4] The Aini people, like some of the other minority ethnic peoples in China and elsewhere in the world, has been abide by a system known as *fuzi-lianming* (father-son linked names), where the last or two syllables of a father's name become the first or first two syllables of his son's name

came to his son's rescue. He ripped the red-cloth headwear from Ge Long's head, tossed it over a bush plant, and ran, dragging Ge Long along with him. Then, something strange happened: the buffalo stopped chasing Ge Long. Instead, it turned to charge at the bushes until it trampled them to the ground. After the incident, Ge Long laughed at the foolhardiness of the buffalo. Poking him on his forehead with a finger, Mang Lege said, "It's you who were being a fool! A startled buffalo hates to see the red color! If I hadn't pulled off your red-cloth headwear, it would have punched so many holes in your body with its horns to make you look like a beehive."

He might get angry with his son and somethings scold him, but Mang Lege loved him very much. The only thing about his son that somewhat let him down was his small stature.

Whenever he talked about it, Mang Lege would say, "I say, son! You may take part of my name and inherit my looks and temperament, but why don't you take after me in terms of my height?"

Ge Long would always respond, "Why do I have to take after you in everything? My height was determined by my mother."

"It was a mistake, a mistake! You should've looked like me, tall and stout, like a real man."

Now, seeing Ge Long suddenly hop in through the window while the company commander was giving orders, Mang Lege shot a glare at him,

"Don't make trouble! We adults are talking business here."

Ge Long stiffened his neck and said, "I'm talking business, too!"

Gu Ming broke into a smile and asked, "What mission are you guaranteeing to accomplish?"

"To go into the forest on a scouting assignment," responded Ge Long blinking his eyes. "I had been overhearing your conversation for a long time outside the door."

"But I didn't assign you any task."

"That's because I didn't come in. Now that I'm here, assign me the task, please."

Before Gu Ming responded, Mang Lege began grabbed Ge Long by his ear, "Beat it! It's not going to a hunting or fishing trip!"

With that, he also picked up a dog-repelling baton and held it vertically with one end on the floor, saying, "What scouting task can you do when you aren't as tall as this?"

Ge Long retorted, "Mom told me that I'll grow taller eventually. Can a dog-repelling baton grow taller?"

Mang Lege fell silent, seething.

Patting Ge Long on his shoulder, Gu Ming said, "You're awesome, Ge Long. You've even stumped up our reconnaissance squad leader with your question!"

Ge Long got hold of Gu Ming's arm and asked, "Awesome or not, just tell me frankly. Are you going to let me go with them?"

"I'm so proud of you for your courage! But you're still a child…"

Without letting Gu Ming finish, he brushed off his arm and grumbled, "A child, a child…"

Before he finished, he leaped out of the window in a flash.

Out of the window, Ge Long caught sight of a figure flickering and then hurrying to hide in a banana grove like a startled muntjac

Ge Long saw it clearly, it was Guo Sha's paternal uncle Ba Muli.

He did not have a good opinion of this skinny old man and somehow felt uncomfortable whenever he saw him walking and trembling like an invalid, holding his own shoulders with his arms crossed.

Forget it! I've neither time nor in the mood to study this sick old man.

Ge Long jumped off the grain-air-drying deck seething and ran across Grandpa Gong Bu walking over.

"Look at you! You bumped into me and almost punched two holes in my stomach like a young bull!"

Grandpa Gong Bu reached out to hold Ge Long in his arms.

Ge Long looked up at Grandpa Gong Bu's broad beaming face.

"Well, Ge Long, you're pouting your lips as far as reaching the sky. Who's offended you?"

Ge Long would not respond, pouting his lips even further.

Grandpa Gong Bu broke into a laugh, "Ha-ha! A cuckoo knows everything that's happening in a forest. You want to participate in their mission of scouting, and Uncle Gu Ming won't let you go, right?"

Now that Grandpa Gong Bu had read his mind, Ge Long nodded with a grievance.

Whenever he had a grievance, he would confide it to Grandpa Gong Bu.

That was because Grandpa Gong Bu had always been nice to him.

Ge Long learned from his ada[5] that when he was young, Grandpa Gong Bu used to be a man that would rather break than bend like himself. For his straightforwardness, he had suffered a lot. He had been single and wandering all his life. He had not settled down in Gehei Village until three years before, when he had turned gray-haired and frail. Though kindless and childless, he was always seen carefree. Known for his kindheartedness, he lent a helping hand to anyone who was in need. Some villagers kindly offered to help him find a wife, but he declined waving his wine gourd.

"Well, I've been living on rice wine and *ganba*[6] all my life. I don't have any wild wish except for being remembered when I die. I would be content if my fellow villagers would

---

[5] "Ada" is an Aini term for "dad"

[6] "Ganba" is beef air dried or baked, a jerky kind of snack preferred by the Aini people

think of me when they observe Asaduo.[7] after I'm buried in the ground."

Ge Long was fond of Grandpa Gong Bu not only because he was a respectful old man or able to tell stories about the forest and wild beasts, but also because he kept a gray black kite.

It was a mighty raptor with strong wings and lustrous eyes.

Grandpa Gong Bu told Ge Long that he had rescued the black kite from its nest under a surprise attack by an old python. At the time, it was still young, pressing its soft wings tight on its back. Grandpa Gong Bu often kept it in his arms. After he settled down in Gehei Village, the black kite had already known to repay his love and care. It flew out of the stilt bamboo house every day and brought back to him in its beak a wild rabbit or a Lady Amherst's pheasant it had caught in the Yuehagu Forest. One day, Grandpa Gong Bu took it with him on a trip to collect mushrooms. When a leopard darted out of the grass to attack him, the black kite swooped down to peck at its eyes and thereby drove it away.

Ge Long liked the black kite very much. He often came to play with it bringing it a mouse he had caught. As soon as he placed the rodent on the ground, the black kite would catch it no matter how fast it scampered.

Grandpa Gong Bu's neighbor Ba Muli, Guo Sha's paternal uncle, often called on him at his stilt bamboo house.

---

[7] An ethnic Aini people's memorial ceremony in honor of their loved ones

Therefore, the black kite was also familiar with Ba Muli and flew into his stilt bamboo house with some game from time to time.

However, five days ago, this cute black kite flew out of Grandpa Gong Bu's bamboo house as usual and never returned.

Grandpa Gong Bu was extremely anxious.

So were Ge Long and Ba Muli.

They looked up into the sky eagerly…

Many black kites flew by, but none descended to alight on Grandpa Gong Bu's stilt bamboo house.

Grandpa Gong Bu lamented, "It got a quick temper. It must have been killed when it tried to catch a wild animal."

Doubtful that the brave black kite could be killed, Ge Long wanted to ask Grandpa Gong Bu some questions. But he bit his tongue when he looked up and saw tears swelling in his eyes.

Ge Long knew how sad Grandpa Gong Bu was about the loss of his beloved black kite. So, he often came to keep him company.

Their relationship was therefore getting stronger with each passing day.

Ge Long was willing to pour his heart out to Grandpa Gong Bu, whether he felt happy or unhappy.

Now, he told Grandpa Gong Bu about his grievances. And, looking into his eyes, he asked, "Grandpa, my ada and Uncle Gu Ming don't want me to go with them on the reconnaissance mission. Do you think they're right?"

"Child," Grandpa Gong Bu held Ge Long in his arms caressing his dark dainty face with a look as gentle as an ocean breeze. He said, "You're still young, as young as a fledgling beginning to learn how to fly. Like a cage with a vicious snake in it, the Yuehagu Forest is not a place for you to set foot in."

"Grandpa Gong Bu, you think I'm too young as well?"

"Child, I don't think you're small at all when you're like a needle used for needlework. But this is a business of cutting down a tree."

"I can become an ax when it comes to cutting down a tree."

"Child, you must listen to the adults. The Yuehagu Forest is too dangerous. Don't you see several scouts have been dispatched one after another, but none has come back?"

"'Child!' 'Child!' You all can say nothing but 'Child!'" With that, Ge Long flounced away.

"This little bullhead!" Grandpa Gong Bu shouted behind him, "Ge Long, your grandpa still has something to say to you!"

Ge Long snorted, thinking, "What else are you going to say except trying to dissuade me to go and compare me to a small needle?"

Grumbling silently, Ge Long did not look back.

Grandpa Gong Bu shook his head and said to himself, "He's now as mad as a bunch of lighted matches."

It was very late that night, but his mother was not home yet.

After smothering the fire in the fire pit, Gulong laid down on the shakedown. Like a cat on a hot tin roof, he could not go to sleep. All he was thinking was his father's early departure tomorrow morning.

Night breeze rustled the areca palm leaves as beautiful as the wings of silver pheasants, bringing whiffs of a song from no one knows where along with the somewhat bitter aroma of the areca flowers into the stilt bamboo house:

Holding our lighted ox-horn torches high,

Oh, we're all here to you saying goodbye!

Oh, you're ours, the Yani[8] people's pride!

A sacrifice-blood-smeared sword on your side,

You're setting off on the bumpy road to stride...

Ge Long learned from his ada that this was an ancient song, a song that told a moving story handed down from their ancestors:

Once upon a time, there was a tree standing by a lake. One day, it suddenly grew wildly, so much so that it blocked the sunlight, thus plunging the earth into total darkness. People could not live on without sunshine. Neither could vegetation survive without sunlight. Therefore, people

---

[8] Yani is what the Aini people call themselves

gathered together to fell the tree with concerted effort. But, replenishing itself as much as it was cut, the tree refused to be cut down. Jimi Jiala, the celestial god, sent a message to Muji, a cultural hero of the Aini people, in his dream, telling him to cut the sky-blocking tree with a sword smeared with the blood of a sacrificed rooster. There was, however, a catch: when the tree was cut down, Muji's life would end simultaneously. Muji was determined to deliver his fellow villagers from the spell of darkness by trading his life for sunlight. Before his departure, the villagers lined up at the exit of their village, holding lighted ox-horn torches pasted with beeswax. While illuminating his way, the villagers sang this tragic and heroic song of farewell.

Lying on the shakedown and listening to the song brought to him by the nightly breeze in staccato, Ge Long suddenly realized that ada was exactly like the hero praised by the song. To keep the village safe, he would venture into the Yuehagu Forest early tomorrow morning.

What about me? Can I follow ada's example?

Ge Long thought and thought, and no one knows how much time had elapsed before he sank his head into the pillow and fell asleep.

He heard the bamboo door creak at midnight.

Opening his eyes, he saw ama[9] coming back home.

He remained quiet.

---

[9] Ama is the Aini dialect for mom.

Ama raised the kerosene hurricane lamp above her head and shone it on the shakedown briefly.

Knowing that ama was checking on him, Ge Long shut his eyes tight in a hurry.

"Ge Long," asked ama gently and tentatively.

Ge Long responded silently, "Ge Long is asleep, Ama."

Thinking that Ge Long was really asleep, ama tiptoed in the room, took a cloth bandana from a bamboo basket hung from the wall, and left, shutting the door quietly behind her.

Whatever ama took with her must be for ada.

Ada and Brother Guo Sha must be getting ready to set out now.

Ge Long could no longer stay put. He sprang up from the shakedown and tagged after ama pussyfooting.

Ama headed straight toward the horse stable in the west of the village on a bumpy road.

Keeping his eyes wide open behind ama, Ge Long saw silhouettes of people flickering in the stable.

When he approached it, he caught sight of many horse-back loads placed in the stable. Each load consisted of two big bamboo baskets of unhusked rice covered with a tarp.

Grandpa Gong Bu was busy loading the last sack of unhusked rice into a basket and covered it up with a tarp.

Gu Ming and Guo Sha checked each of the horseback loads to make sure all were tied securely.

Aha, Ge Long understood...

Ada and Brother Guo Sha would leave at dawn under the guise of grain merchants. They would set off leading a horse caravan through the Yuehagu Forest.

Ge Long was secretly delighted at his inference when suddenly something rustled in the banana grove.

He spotted a skinny figure sneaking out tottering and furtively disappearing in the darkness of the night.

It was Ba Muli!

What was he doing here?

Ge Long had not found any time to ruminate what was happening when he heard ada's voice coming from the stable: "Alright! Don't worry! Everything's ready!"

Ge Long quickly directed his eyes toward the stable and saw ama handing the cloth bandana to ada.

"There's clothing in it. When you're soaked in the rain, you can change into it."

Ada asked ama in a hushed voice, "Is Ge Long fast asleep?"

"Yes, he is."

"He nagged me during the day, asking me to take him along. To be frank, I'd like him to venture out and see the world. Our son is always bent on doing something if he sets his mind on it. He won't care even if the sky collapses because of it."

"He's like you!"

"Neither the company leader nor I give him our consent, so he took offence. The company leader is going to have a talk with him. So, please chime in on my behalf."

Mang Lege, tomorrow, you...."

"Look at you! What's happening to you?"

"......"

"Well, well, looks like you need to be talked to first."

"I don't need it. Aren't you going to fine-tune your plans before you go? I'll excuse myself and go home."

Upon hearing his ama's words, Ge Long sneaked away.

When she returned home, ama found Ge Long fast asleep, huddling into a ball like a lazy kitty on the shakedown.

Chapter 3

Jingling, jingling, and jingling…

The clear and melodious bells of the horse caravan disturbed the verdant dream of the valley of Mount Nuocha.

As it woke up, the valley yawned, breathing out a gust of chilly breeze, which drifted over from the depth of the thick, shaded foliage.

Dewdrops woke up and twinkled their glistening eyes on the grass blades; birds woke up and, fluttering and hopping, vied with one another in singing the first morning song; the forests and groves woke up and, as soon as they combed their hairy branches and twigs, they powdered themselves with the rosy morning glow.

A red deer that had just rinsed its antlers trotted out of the stripestem fernleaf bamboo grove on its slender legs and fixed its alarmed eyes on the train of horses traveling in the patchy fog.

Jingling, jingling, jingling...

Leading the caravan was an old black horse that knew the way.

On its forehead was tied a round mirror laced with red cloth. It glistened and glared as it vacillated.

No one knows when the Aini people started to put a mirror on the head of the leading horse and gave it an amazing name: "a demon detector." It had since become a tradition. Each time they travel in a caravan, the Aini people would put a round mirror on the leading horse's forehead. They hoped that the flashing light reflected from the mirror would drive away all evil spirits on their way to keep them and their horses from harm's way.

Shouldering heavy responsibility, this old black horse walked unhurriedly with two baskets full of unhusked rice over its back, nine bells jingling beneath its neck.

Following the old black horse, Guo Sha tapped at its dock irregularly with a bamboo stick he was twiddling in his hand.

As he was traveling, he deliberately wore a new set of clothes: a blue cloth shirt and a pair of loose black pants of homespun cloth.

A train of about two dozen rice-carrying horses traveled in a sometimes close and sometimes loose file. But they all loyally followed the old black horse with the bells jingling beneath its neck.

Mang Lege brought the rear. He was wearing a black shirt and a pair of black pants with a trailing-pointed knife on his waist. He scanned at the low-lying bushes of undulating crowns from time to time.

By noon, the horse caravan had left the mountain valley and arrived at the bank of the Lanmang River. The Yuehagu Forest lay on the other side.

The Lanmang River was flanked by undulating, round-leafed bushes. The river was about twenty-five to thirty meters wide and of varying depth in different sections. It could be fathomless where it was the deepest. Someone caught sight of an old catfish swimming to the surface from the bottom to bask in the sun, the top of its head alone appearing as big as a bamboo basket. Where the water was the shallowest, the water reached only to the knee. One could simply wade through by rolling up the legs of pants.

The leading old black horse arrived at the shallow part of the river and splashed into it.

A timid gray pony balked snorting behind it.

"Go on! Don't be afraid!"

Guo Sha dragged it into the water by the reigns.

As soon as its hooves touched the bottom of the river, the gray pony pulled itself together and went to catch up with the old black horse.

Funneling his strength into his soles, Guo Sha firmly stepped on the riverbed mossy pebbles and kept abreast with the pace of the gray pony.

The little fish struggling against the current rallied around his feet and nipping at them, thus making him feel itchy.

When they waded to the middle of the river, the old black horse suddenly stumbled and fell neighing.

Weighed down by the loads, it failed to stand up after struggling a while. On the contrary, it was carried quite a distance by the rapids.

"The horse fell! The horse fell!"

Guo Sha screamed with alarm.

Before the sound of Guo Sha's scream died away, a crocodile emerged rolling from the splashing water, revealing its inky back and then submerged for hiding.

It turned out that the old black horse had stepped upon the crocodile lurking on the riverbed, treating it as a rock.

Feeling hurt, the crocodile had rolled over and, in doing so, thrown the old black horse off its balance.

While screaming, Guo Sha rushed over to help the old black horse up. But, in a hurry, he lost his foothold and fell as well.

"Take hold of the reins. I'm coming!"

Mang Lege hurried over yelling, his feet splattering the water. But the pebbles were so slippery that he also fell and rolled over a few times on the riverbed.

With a tremendous effort, they finally helped the old black horse up in the rapids.

Shaking off the muddy water from its body, the old black horse led the caravan across the Lanmang River.

The two men were dog-tired, their limbs wrapped tight in their wet clothes.

"Aha! Knowing we're too warm from walking, the god of earth A'ao'apo gave us a cold shower!"

Mang Lege walked up the sand beach. As he joked laughing, he unbuttoned his soaked shirt and pants.

Wiping the beads of water from his face, Guo Sha said, "So, we have to thank this old deity, right?"

"Right! When we make a profit from this trip, we'll buy two hams and a gourd of rice wine and offer them to him as a sacrifice."

"Great. If only we could return safely!"

"Yes, if only. Come, Guo Sha. Let's sundry our clothes and take a break."

As he said so, Mang Lege had taken off his clothes, baring his swarthy, sinewy muscles. He produced an iron box from his pocket, shook his shirt and pants open, and spread them over the bushes by the river to dry them in the sun. He then plopped down on the sand. Opening the iron box, he took out a small piece of binlang of tobacco mixed with rukh pipla, put it in the mouth, and began to chew it. Before long, purplish juice seeped from the corner of his mouth. He felt really refreshed.

Guo Sha also took off his shirt and pants and spread them over the bushes for sundry. He then asked Mang Lege for a piece of his binlang, stuff it into his mouth, and started chewing. Meanwhile, he lay down on his back and sprawled on the sand beach to rest himself with his eyes closed.

The wind from the river swayed the bushes, bringing gusts of cool air to the stark-naked men. From time to time, one or two little egrets flew over the Lanmang River into the Yuehagu Forest, flapping their snow-white wings as they made "kre-kre-kre" calls.

Mang Lege squinted at the horse-caravan path overgrown with cogon grass.

In the middle of this horse-caravan path traversing the forest, there was a caravansary known as "Black Gem." It was an inn that served caravan leaders exclusively. Its owner was named You Mansa.

Without encountering the bandits on their way, they can get to the caravansary before the setting sun touched the mountaintop. Mang Lege mumbled to himself.

However, the bandits will by no means spare such a train of horses fully loaded with rice. Who knows what would be in store for the caravan once it was in the Yuehagu Forest…?

"Oh, gosh! My clothes! My clothes!"

Guo Sha's abrupt scream interrupted Mang Lege's contemplation.

He turned to look and found Guo Sha picking himself up hurriedly and darting toward the bushes while shouting. He reached his hands out and managed to get hold of his black cloth pants that had nearly blown into the river by the wind. But his blue cloth shirt had long gone.

Mang Lege sprang up and rushed to grab his shirt and pants. As he lay his hands on them, he felt them light and dry.

"Well, my shirt has become fish food!"

Guo Sha gazed at the lower reaches of the river for a long time. Finally, he gave up any hope.

Mang Lege went up to him and draped his own black cloth shirt over his shoulders.

"Come, put this on."

"No, I can't. If I wore yours, what would you wear?"

"Of course, I'm not going to visit the Yuehagu Forest half-naked."

As he said so, Mang Lege walked toward the yellow young horse with a load of miscellaneous items. From a basket, he pulled out the bandana that his wife had handed to him. He opened it and took out a blue-cloth shirt. He flaunted it to Guo Sha.

Guo Sha was surprised.

Mang Lege burst into a laughter.

"Ha-ha! Now you see, this is the benefit of having a wife, isn't it?" With that, he put the blue-cloth shirt on.

After they fixed themselves up, they spurred the horses on with verbal commands and headed toward the Yuehagu Forest.

Young trees were lying low densely on the outskirt of the forest, as if they were escaping with life, vying with one another in getting out of the perennially dark forest.

Through the low-lying young trees, the forest became

thicker and thicker.

The green umbrella-like crowns of the tall trees overlapped one another and formed a gigantic natural canopy.

The canopy was not so tightly woven that it had cracks to allow sunlight to peep in. Those parasitic plants of various kinds crawled as high as they could to fight for the sunlight leaking through the foliage. Once exposed to sunlight, they began to expand aggressively in all directions in order to fill the cracks in the canopy.

Therefore, sunlight was no longer available in the depth of the forest.

Fortunately, the old black horse knew where he was heading. Swaying its jingle bells, it walked toward the destination of which it was confident.

Suddenly, Guo Sha let out a horrifying scream: "Ouch!"

And he fell thumping to the ground like a hitching post that had been cut down. His limbs were jerking spasmodically.

Mang Lege was stunned. He dashed toward Guo Sha, scooped his upper body up, and held him in his arms.

A knife had been planted in Guo Sha's back!

A tailing-pointed knife with double edges!

Mang Lege immediately knew what had happened:

Bandits!

He surveyed around with his eyes wide open.

It was pitch dark all around. And it was deadly silent, too.

Where did the knife fly from?

Suddenly, Mang Lege spotted an eerie eye above his head gazing at him without blinking.

It gave him a shudder.

Taking a closer look, he found an owl.

"Growl! Growl!"

Guo Sha groaned miserably.

His tanned face looked as if it were covered with a sheet of white paper.

"Guo Sha! Guo Sha!"

Mang Lege kept calling his name.

Seeing Guo Sha's face distorted with pain, he had the urge to pull the knife out.

But he decided not to, and he was not supposed to.

He knew if he did so, blood would gush out from the wound.

Once the blood was let out, Guo Sha would die at once.

Just then, the owl on the tree gave off an unearthly cry:

"Hooooo…"

Following the cry, it fluttered its wings in panic and fled into the depth of the forest.

With the flight of the owl, a burly man appeared from behind an old thorn tree like an aspiration.

This unanticipated burly man had a fierce-looking, swarthy face, with caterpillar-like brows above a pair of eagle-like eyes ablaze with menace. Tramping nonchalantly on the thorny twigs covering the ground with his broad feet, he walked waddling toward Mang Lege.

Mang Lege cast a glance at him, concluding that he must have been one of the bandits he was looking for.

If he had let his temper get the best of him, he would have jumped to the little yellow horse a moment before and pulled the Mauser C96 out of the basket and sprayed the bandit with all the bullets in its magazine.

But he managed to rein in his temper.

He even kept the fire of anger in his eyes from showing because he was conscious of his faked identify as a caravan leader.

But he pretended to be in panic and, trembling all over, backed a few steps closer to the yellow young horse.

The bandit did not seem to take Mang Lege seriously.

He went up to Guo Sha, grabbed him by his collar, and pulled his upper body off the ground.

He took a glance at Guo Sha's ghastly face, snorted, and let go of him. Guo Sha thumped back to the ground again.

Turning around, he grinned at Mang Lege, baring his black teeth, "Hehe, he's done for!"

Before Mang Lege responded, the hideously grinning bandit reached his big, black hand toward Mang Lege and demanded, "Hand it to me!"

What? What's he demanding of me? Mang Lege's heart was thumping like a drum in his chest.

Pretending to be fearful and confused, he asked back dumbly, "What, what are you're asking of me?"

The bandit unexpectedly burst into a laughter, "Hehe! Hehe!"

He laughed a while before ordering again with his eyes wide open, "Give me the secret letter!"

What? A secret letter?!

Now, Mang Lege was really confused.

"Stopping playing the fool! Come on! Give me the secret letter to Boss Mansa!"

While Mang Lege was at a loss, Guo Sha suddenly shrieked. He wriggled like a snake and grabbed the bandit's ankle in his hands.

The bandit was panicked, regarding Guo Sha as his ghost. He tried desperately to free himself from his grip.

Guo Sha went crazy and sank his teeth into the bandit's ankle.

Taking this opportunity, Mang Lege inched even closer to the yellow young horse.

He decided to pull the gun out and capture the bandit alive so as to get to the bottom of this secret letter to Boss Mansa.

Guo Sha burst into crying all of a sudden, "You stabbed the wrong man! You stabbed the wrong man…"

At this, both Mang Lege and the bandit were stunned.

Pointing at his black-cloth waistband with his trembling hand, Guo Sha squeezed a few indistinct words between his quivering lips:

"It's in… It's in…"

Before he could finish, he spouted a mouthful of purple

blood, rolled up his eyes, and stopped breathing.

The bandit took a quick look at Mang Lege, bent over skeptical, and began to fumble at Guo Sha's waist.

As he had expected, he felt something. Hurriedly did he untie the waistband and took out a thumb-size bamboo tube.

Aware of the imminent danger, Mang Lege immediately pulled the gun out from the bamboo basket.

He was about to level the gun when he heard the bandit shouting,

"Here goes my knife!"

Whish…

A sharp, lancet-like throwing knife flew from the bandit's sleeve with a flash.

Quick of eyes and nimble of body, Mang Lege dodged the knife by throwing himself onto the ground and sliding to the other side of the yellow young horse from under it.

Thud! The knife hit the basket.

Hiding behind the horse load, Mang Lege cocked the hammer of the gun with a "click," and pointed it at the bandit, shouting,

"Don't move! If you do, I'll pop your head!"

The bandit opened his eagle-like eyes as big as one of the bells under the horse's neck.

Looking into the dark barrel, he panted hard.

Suddenly, he ripped open his black-cloth shirt with both hands to reveal his hairy chest.

In the tiger-skin belt at least fifteen centimeters wide

worn tight on his waist, there were a row of trailing-pointed knives glittering coldly.

Patting his chest with his palm, the bandit shouted, "Aim here and shoot!"

The guy's death-defying attitude put Mang Lege in a dilemma.

To keep him alive for more information, then I can't shoot and kill him; to injure him by firing at his limbs, then the gunshots would attract the bandits to him.

While Mang Lege faltered, the bandit pulled two knives out, one in each hand, and yelling like a demon, threw himself upon Mang Lege hiding behind the horse.

Before the bandit approached him, Mang Lege put his gun back in his waist and pushed the horse loads hard.

The yellow young horse lost its balance and, with the loads on its back, fell toward the bandit.

The momentum of the horse knocked the bandit off balance as well, so that he staggered back a few steps in a row.

Taking advantage of this favorable situation, Mang Lege jumped over the yellow young horse and threw himself upon the bandit.

The bandit hoisted the knives in his hands even before he managed to come to a stop.

Mang Lege grasped the bandit by his wrists with both his hands and held them back abruptly so that the two knives were up in the air in the bandit's hands. Meanwhile, Mang Lege stretched his neck and thrusted his head up and bumped the bandit in his lower jaw. Unprepared for such a quick move, the bandit bit his tongue hard and gave a scream of pain. Losing no time, Mang Lege pulled his left thigh up and hit the bandit in his lower abdomen with the knee. The strike sent the bandit bending over, letting go his knives, and falling to the ground on his back with a thud. Mang Lege then threw himself upon him while reaching out his hands and put them around his neck.

The bandit was so suffocated that he showed the whites of his eyes.

Suddenly, he puffed up his cheeks and spat out a mouthful of gross blood mixed with saliva, as well as the part of the tongue he had bitten off—all onto Mang Lege's face.

The sticky and stench blood mixture blinded Mang Lege for a moment.

Mang Lege spontaneously let go one of his hands to wipe the blood off his eyes. Seizing the opportunity, the bandit punched him hard in his cheek.

Struck off balance, Mang Lege rolled off the bandit.

After knocking Mang Lege to the ground, the bandit arched his lower back and sprang up. At the same time, he pulled another two knives from his waist and pounced upon Mang Lege. Holding his knives high, he was ready to thrust them into Mang Lege.

But before the tips of his knives reached Mang Lege, the latter pushed his two hands up and drove a tailing-pointed knife in each hand into the bandit's stomach simultaneously.

Giving a blood-curdling scream, the bandit loosened his knives and collapsed to the ground.

It turned out that when Mang Lege had been punched in the cheek by the bandit, he had deliberately rolled off him. At that time, he caught sight of the two knives that the former had unwittingly thrown onto the ground when he had fallen. He had grabbed them aa soon as his hands touched the ground. Now, with them, he stabbed the bandit when the latter was throwing himself upon him again.

Mang Lege killed the desperado who had refused to surrender. He shook his head, regretting that he was not able to capture him alive so that he could have otherwise gotten some useful information from him.

He turned the bandit over and searched his body. He found the bamboo tube in his pocket.

Mang Lege examined the bamboo tube held in his hand and found in it a tiny roll of banana leaf, which looked like a small stick.

Ah, needless to say, this is the secret letter to be delivered to Boss Mansa.

Mang Lege was about to take out the banana-leaf roll from the bamboo tube when suddenly he sensed a whiff of wind coming from nowhere. Before he had a chance to look back, he heard a bang and felt a thick chestnut club hitting the back of his head with great velocity.

A fog of sudden pain cloaked his vision, and he dropped to the ground unconscious.

A shaggy-faced man cast away the chestnut club and gave Mang Lege a kick. When he saw that Mang Lege's body was limp, he crouched down, pried his hand open, and took the bamboo tube away.

The shaggy-faced man put the bamboo tube into the leather box around his waist. He then took out a coil of coir rope, shook it open, and unhurriedly tied the fainted Mang Lege securely. Then he ripped a piece from the shirt of the swarthy-faced bandit and rammed it in Mang Lege's mouth.

After he finished, he picked a big horse, unloaded the packs from its back, and led it toward Mang Lege.

Apparently, he was going to put Mang Lege on the horseback and take him somewhere.

He dragged and pulled Mang Lege's saggy body, trying to carry him onto the back of the horse with a tremendous effort...

When, "whoosh," there came flying...

A sharp arrow, which hit the shaggy-faced man right in his left temple.

And it entered it and went out of the right temple. It was a through and through.

What a sharp archer!

How powerful the archer was!

The shaggy-faced man fell still onto the ground without giving a whimper.

Four men were lying under the old thorn tree now.

This sudden turn of event threw the train of horses into disorder.

Opening their eyes wide in panic, they bumped into one another while snorting and digging restlessly.

A Chestnut seemed to be the only one that remained calm in the commotion.

It stood firmly there, head raised high, watching what was happening in front of its sparkling eyes.

Before long, the tarp covering one of the baskets on its back was lifted up, and from underneath it crawled out a dark-complexioned child.

Ah, it was Ge Long!

How had Ge Long ended up in the basket?

It was a long story...

Ge Long, bent on going with his ada on this scouting mission, had had a hard time going to sleep that night. As soon as the day broke, he got off the shakedown, armed himself with the bow and arrows, said goodbye to his sleeping ama silently, pussyfooted out of the stilt bamboo house, and sneaked into the stable.

He poured the unhusked rice out of one of the baskets, hid it somewhere in the stable, and crawled into the basket, where he concealed himself. He then followed the caravan out of the village in the dewy morning.

He meant to crawl out after the caravan crossed the Lanmang River and entered the Yuehagu Forest.

Then, his ada would be unable to shoo him back even if he wanted to.

Ha-ha! Small stature had its benefit. If he had been big, the basket would have been too small for him.

After the horse caravan left the village, Ge Long was so excited about his success that he was trembling slightly all over.

However, before long, the swaying basket on the horseback gradually turned into a cradle.

And the sound of the clanging horse bells became a monotonous lullaby.

Ge Long, who had been up all night, now was as drowsy as a little Lady Amherst's pheasant chick. Holding the crossbow in his arms and curling himself into a ball, he eventually fell into a slumber.

When he opened his eyes, he felt that Chestnut stopped moving forward. On the contrary, it had planted his hoofs squarely on the ground.

Where is this?

Why isn't Chestnut moving?

Ge Long gingerly lifted the tarp covering his head and peeped out. Yikes! He barely cried out.

In sight was a large pool of blood with Guo Sha and a dark-faced man lying in it.

A shaggy-faced man was throwing a coir rope around ada, trying to bind him.

Gee? What happened to ada?

Why does he allow this shaggy-faced man to tie him up?

Ge Long soon realized that ada was unconscious.

His eyes burning with anger, he leveled his crossbow and, seizing the right moment, shot the arrow at the target he was aiming at: the temple of the shaggy-faced man.

The man was rendered motionless.

Ge Long had clambered out of the bamboo basket and ran toward his ada.

"Ada! Ada!"

Ge Long cut off the coir rope binding his ada.

"Ada! Ada!"

Ge Long shook his Ada hard.

Mang Lege did not respond.

Ge Long was so worried that he burst into tears.

He unfastened a gourd filled with water from the horse-back.

Splash! He poured the gourd-full of water upon his ada's face.

The sudden chill of the water woke Mang Lege up from his unconsciousness. Now he was alert enough to hear someone calling him.

He opened his eyes, only to see the teary face of his son.

The sight was beyond his expectation.

"Ge Long!"

"Ada!"

"Why are you here?"

"I'm here to rescue you."

Rescue me? Instantly, Mang Lege, who had regained consciousness, recalled everything that had happened.

"You're great!"

"I've been great all the time. It's a shame you know it only now!"

'Yes, but I know it only now." With that, Mang Lege broke into a laughter.

Picking up the Mauser C96, Mang Lege stuck it in his belt and then removed the bamboo tube from the shaggy-faced man's leather box.

"What's it?" asked Ge Long, his eyes blinking.

"I want to know what it is myself."

As he said so, Mang Lege shook the roll of banana leaf out of the tube and unfurled it cautiously.

On the banana leaf, two lines of text are carved with the tip of a knife:

> **"Get rid of the Black Plague!**
>
> **Ask the messenger for details.**
>
> **Ba"**

After reading the secret letter, Mang Lege knitted his brows:

Apparently the text "Get rid of the Black Plague" means to kill me.

That's because I was wearing all back whereas Guo Sha was wearing a blue shirt and a pair of black pants when we set out.

He became the fall guy only because he switched into my clothes after he fell into the stream and got soaked.

No wonder Big Liu and other scouts were never able to return from their missions…

A secret letter reached the bandits as soon as they set off on their trip.

"Ask the messenger for details" sounds like the messenger must be Guo Sha.

As a matter of fact, Guo Sha was a spy working for the bandits!

"For details…" What are the details then?

What would Guo Sha tell the bandits?

From analyzing the two sentences, it follows that I would be killed after the secret letter were delivered to the recipient. But why did the dark-faced bandit act prematurely before it was delivered?

"Ba" must be the writer of the letter.

Then, what's the rest of the name with "Ba"?

In Gehei Village, at least more than a dozen people have names beginning with the "Ba."

There are also lots of villagers who have "Ba" in the middle or at the end of their names.

Quite a few faces of the villagers with "Ba" in their names flashed before Mang Lege's mind's eye.

But soon, he thought of someone who had asked Guo Sha to deliver the secret letter. It was none other than Guo Sha's paternal uncle Ba Muli, the sickly-looking, small old man.

Ge Long broke the silence, saying, "Ada, as for this 'Ba,' could it be Ba Muli?"

"Why do you think so?"

"He's Guo Sha's paternal uncle."

"Just because of this?"

"No, there's something more. When Uncle Gu Ming assigned you this task yesterday, Ba Muli seemed to eavesdrop leaning over the stilt bamboo house outside. I saw him when I jumped out. Besides, when you were filling the sacks with unhusked rice, I ran into him, too. He is always being evasive…"

"Oh?!"

As he fixed his eyes on the secret letter, Mang Lege heard the deep and gruff voice of the black-faced bandit ringing in his ears:

"Come on! Give me the secret letter to Boss Mansa!"

Yes, Boss Mansa must be the recipient of the secret letter.

If it's not a namesake, it must be the manager of the Black Gem caravansary…

After serious consideration, Mang Lege made up his mind.

He said to Ge Long sparkling his eyes, "Okay, you can come with me now!"

"Don't you think I'm too short?"

"Well, being short can be an advantage in the right situation!"

Ge Long smiled cheerfully.

"Let's leave here immediately!"

"Where for?"

"The Black Gem caravansary.

Chapter 4

Pu Linuo, the guy at the Black Gem caravansary, came out and greeted the father and son with a smile on his face.

Blinking his small but piercing eyes, he said to the guests coming to stay in a raised voice:

"Hey, here come a horse, a father, and a son. It goes without asking that you are visiting your kith and kin across the border, aren't you? Please take a rest in our stilt bamboo house. As a saying goes, "The fragrance of beautiful flowers attracts butterflies; the bouquet of good wine appeals to new guests." I've just opened a barrel of red-rice wine, and now guests begin to stream in. We haven't been so busy at the Black Gem caravansary for a long time!"

The father and son whom Pu Linuo treated as passerby guests were none other than Mang Lege and Ge Long.

They had tied some stones to the bodies of Guo Sha and the other two bandits and sunk them into the Lanmang River. Mang Lege chose Chestnut and unloaded its pack. He then turned the old black horse who knew the way toward the direction of Gehei Village and let it lead the caravan back to it, with the "demon-detecting mirror" bobbing on its nodding head when it was walking or trotting. Watching the train of horses wading smoothly across the Lanmang River, Mang Lege reached out to pick Ge Long up and placed him on the horseback with him.

Mang Lege was certainly not unarmed. He had a Mauser C96 and two stick grenades.

In a period when three bowls of tobacco would have been burned to ashes by a smoker, Chestnut carried them to the Black Gem caravansary.

"Here, I'll take your horse! We've got water and high-quality fodder in the stable. Besides, I get up at midnight to add fodder. I'll guarantee that when you set out tomorrow morning, you'll find your Chestnut in high spirits."

While saying so, Pu Linuo reached out for the reins.

"What you said is like the wind blowing in the valley, cooling your heat-suffering guests off!" Mang Lege handed the reins to Pu Linuo and carried Ge Long off the horseback, saying, "Get off, son. Now that we have come to a hospitable host, we don't have to listen to the roars of leopards while sitting under a big tree in the wild tonight."

Pointing at the stilt bamboo house, Pu Linuo asked the father and son to rest as he led Chestnut to the stable in the backyard.

Mang Lege took Ge Long by hand and climbed up the stairs. When he pushed the door open, he caught sight of five or six passerby guests sitting around drinking rice wine.

On the bamboo floor, there was a wide and round wood barrel, which was carved out of a single thick tree trunk. The bung hole on the top of the barrel was stopped up by a bung, which was pleated of rice straw. A few curved bamboo tubes were inserted into the bung.

Those who sat around the barrel was each holding the end of a bamboo tube in his hand. They were sucking up the red-rice wine from the wood barrel.

One of the tubes was especially long, so much so that it reached to the far end of the shakedown. On it, a man was reclining with his head on a bedroll. Crossing one leg on the other and half closing his eyes, he was holding the bamboo tube in both hands. He was sucking the wine unhurriedly with enjoyment. He shook his crossed leg a bit when he felt particularly content.

The ethnic Aini people have a saying, "Drinking is part of an important ritual." Therefore, wine must be served on big occasions such as celebrating festivals, entertaining guests, and having parties. Each household knows how to brew their rice wine with boiled millets fermented with yeast in a wood barrel. All of the Aini people, man and woman, are good drinkers.

Seeing Mang Lege and his son stepping in, the guests drinking around the barrel spread out politely.

A stout man with a big opening mouth even stood up and handed a spare bamboo tube to Mang Lege.

"I say, brother, come and drink a few mouthfuls to refresh yourself. Boss Mansa's red-rice wine is sweeter than honey."

Before Mang Lege expressed his thankfulness, Ge Long looked into the eyes of the big-opening-mouth guy and asked, "Why don't you invite me to drink?"

"A little kid like you also want to drink wine, eh? I'm afraid you might wet your pants if you did!" Big Opening Mouth jeered and burst into a guffaw.

The rest of the guests echoed with an uproar of laughter.

"Argh, don't you look down upon me!"

With that, Ge Long yanked the bamboo tube away from Big Opening Mouth's hand and sucked quite a few big mouthful of the wine. Then, raising his head and pointing at the man's face, he began to comment his features,

"These are your eyes. This is your nose. These are your ears, and this is your big mouth, aren't they?"

This time, his retort set the guests laughing wildly with the compliments, "You're really a good drinker! Really a good drinker!"

Ge Long felt encouraged and continued, "I could drink up the wine in the whole barrel but I just don't want to kill your joy!"

The guy who crossed his legs on the shakedown put down his leg and made an effort to lift his heavy eye lids weighed down by slight inebriety and said, "Since you're such a drinker, you were brought up with wine, weren't you?"

"Yes, you guessed right!" Ge Long replied, patting his chest with confirmation.

"Let me be frank with you all, brothers. It's me who fed him wine when he was a baby. When he was still breastfed, his mother and I had to work in the fields, and we had to leave him behind at home. To prevent him from toddling around and hurting himself, we had to give him a mouthful or so of the wine to put him out. As time goes by, well, this little rascal has become a drinker who doesn't know what drunkenness is."

Mang Lege's explanation made the guests laugh again.

All the passerby guests soon became communicable friends.

Big Opening Mouth took a few mouthfuls of the wine and heaved a big sigh.

"Since the arrival of the bandits, we find it more and more difficult to travel on this path."

"That's true!" said the man reclining on the shakedown with deep empathy, "One day, I just bought a batch of waist knives of high-quality steel and planned to sell them to the villagers for a good price. When I stayed in this caravansary, Boss Mansa discovered my knives. He tried his best to persuade me to discard them lest they fell into the bandits' hands. I really hated to lose the capital money I had spent on purchasing the knives, so I didn't listen. Boss Mansa said nothing. Who would have expected that several masked bandits came to rob the caravansary at midnight? I panicked and shivered all over. But guess what? The bandits searched my horse packs thoroughly, but they found no knives in them at all! I was equally stunned at the time. I knew for sure I had placed the knives in the packs, and how come the bandits couldn't find them? Only after the bandits left did I learn that Boss Mansa had put them away. But for Boss Mansa's help, I could have fallen a victim to the swords of the bandits."

"Speaking of Boss Mansa, he's really a hard-to-find good man," said a man with a mole on his forehead. "Once, when I stayed in the caravansary, I saw with my own eyes how he helped an elderly guest conceal his grain in his cellar. That day, bandits happened to raid and beat Boss Mansa to a pulp, but he never gave up the grain."

"Hey, did you hear," Big Opening Mouth swept a glance at everyone mysteriously and said in a hushed voice, "I heard the bandit-suppressing troops are coming this way to fight the bandits. Like fish that have leapt on the bank, the bandits' days are numbered!"

They were chit-chatting when the bamboo house's wooden staircase creaked. A man pushed the door open and entered.

This man was in his fifties and short. He had a plump, round face, with a pair of bright round eyes, a bulbous nose, and a circle beard with the moustache and chin hair connected and wrapping around his mouth. He wore a black cloth headwear, a short shirt and a pair long pants, both of washed-out blue coarse cloth. He was holding a big bamboo pipe in his left hand and an incense stick giving out black smoke in his right.

As soon as he entered, all those who knew him stood up to greet him in courtesy,

"Boss Mansa!"

Knowing that this was Boss Mansa, Mang Lege rose pulling Ge Long up at the same time.

Boss Mansa waved the guests to sit down while beaming. He then pulled out a small, round, rattan stool and sat on it opposite Mang Lege. He produced a flat iron tobacco box from his waist, took a pinch of the golden cut tobacco from it, and lit it with the incense stick. Putting his mouth to the lip of the big bamboo pipe, he took a deep puff so that the water in the tube gurgled on and off. The tobacco in the bowl flicked brightly a few times and turned into ashes.

Boss Mansa looked up, exhaled a mouthful of smoke contently, and ping-ponged his squinted eyes from Mang Lege and Ge Long before he unhurriedly asked, "Pu Linuo told me about the arrival of new guests. I think they must be you, a father and son. Am I right?"

Mang Lege nodded and replied, "Like exhausted birds, we are here to perch and rest in your bamboo house."

"He-he!" Boss Mansa's face glowed with chuckles. "By bestowing a black gem to me, the A'ao'abo god meant for me to serve my guests well. Well, you haven't had your supper yet, have you?"

Patting his abdomen, Ge Long said, "You're right. My belly began to rumble as if there were a little frog croaking in it."

"Well, well, well, you'd better not let it jump out of your mouth. Pu Linuo is going to bring your food here."

After he finished, he directed his eyes toward Mang Lege and asked, "Are you visiting your relatives and friends?"

"Yes. My brother had someone send me a message, saying that he was going to be married and inviting me to his wedding."

"Wow, that's great!" Boss Mansa refilled his pipe with some cut tobacco and continued, "Riding on your horse, you two must have traveled pretty fast. Did you run into any bandits on your way?"

Mang Lege said smiling, "Thanks to A'ao'abo's for his blessings, we were safe and sound all the way."

As he puffed, Boss Mansa raised his head and cast a look at the rear window. "It's getting late. Not sure if there're still horse caravans out there on the path. Well, did you encounter any?"

Mang Lege replied "No, we didn't," his eyes blinking.

Boss Mansa nodded, "Well, that's good. It's not safe on this path. As a manager of the caravansary, I'm always feeling worried about my guests."

Just then, Pu Linuo brought food over.

Boss Mansa rose and said goodnight.

Before he left, he looked around at the stilt bamboo house and told Pu Linuo,

"It's pretty crowded here. Don't we have vacant rooms at the back? Take the father and son there, please."

"Consider it done!"

Pu Linuo nodded and set the dishes on the table.

The dishes were scrumptious, including snow-white glutinous rice, fried preserved pork slices, dried little fish, pickled bamboo shoots, and beef jerky.

After supper, Mang Lege and Ge Long followed Pu Linuo out of the bamboo house to the backyard.

The backyard was overgrown with lush banana trees, one cluster after another, forming a wind-tight grove.

Behind the broad banana leaves were three or four low-lying stilt bamboo houses independent of each other.

Pu Linuo led the father and son through the banana grove. Amid the banana trees there erected a huge mushroom-shaped rock, with a spring gurgling beneath it. The water was up to the rim of the pool but did not seem to overflow.

Pu Linuo said, "Look, this is the black gem A'ao'abo bestowed to our Boss Mansa. If you drink the spring water beneath it, you'll have a long life with never-graying hair."

Ge Long was fascinated and asked, "So you drink from this spring every day?"

"Yes, I do."

"So, you can live a long, long life!"

"Ha-ha! I've lived a long life already. I started to work for Boss Mansa when I was your age. If it were not for this precious stone, he would have relocated long ago. Who'd like to run a hotel business here with his heart in his mouth every day?"

Mang Lege chimed in, "You're right. It's really risky to have a hotel business here."

"I say, it's said that the bandit-suppressing troops are coming this way. Is that true?" asked Pu Linuo staring into Mang Lege's eyes.

Mang Lege nodded, "I've also heard about it."

"I heard that the bandit-suppressing troops are already stationed in Gehei Village."

"Are you sure? I just passed by the village and didn't see any. I didn't hear of the villagers talk about them, either.

"I see." Pu Linuo stopped asking.

He took the father and son to one of the low-lying stilt bamboo houses and left after saying goodnight.

This was a bamboo house used for storage of sundries. The walls and ceiling were blackened by the soot and smoke from the fire pit. The corners were covered with spider webs. The floor was covered with a rough bamboo mat. The baskets, pots, and jars stacked on the floor took a large share of the bamboo house's space. A piece of white wood whittled and hacked unevenly lay on the floor, used as a dividing line between the floor space and the shakedown. The latter was not big but very clean and tidy. On a white sheet there were two rolls of beddings of flowery patterns. Compared with the miscellaneous items with dust accumulated on them, the shakedown seemed to be a totally different world.

Mang Lege took off his shoes, lay on his back on the shakedown, and closed his eyes.

The caterpillar-like eyebrows were knitted together.

Is this manager of the caravansary the recipient of the secret letter?

He doesn't seem to be so the way he talked and was complimented by the passerby guests.

Can he be just a namesake?

Where is another Boss Mansa hiding?

Knowing that something was weighing on his ada's mind, Ge Long climbed up to the shakedown quietly and lay on his stomach beside him in silence.

After a while, Ge Long could not keep quiet anymore. He extended his neck a bit so that his face was against ada's chin.

"Ada."

"Yes?"

"This Boss Mansa doesn't look like a bad guy."

"Why?"

"Everybody speaks highly of him."

"Just because of this?"

"There's more…"

"More what?"

"Well, I've been observing him in secret, and the more I see him, the less likely he's a bad guy."

Mang Lege raised his upper body and held his son's dainty face in his big hand.

"Then, what do you think about Guo Sha? He was not bad?"

"Guo Sha?"

Ge Long was speechless.

"Ge Long, lie here stay put. I'll go out and take a look."

"I'll go with you."

"No, you can't."

"Yes, I can."

"Do you know who you are now?"

"Your son."

"Wrong!"

"Then who am I?"

"Now you are my soldier, and I'm your commander. You must obey my orders."

"…alright."

Mang Lege rose, yanked out the stick grenades from his belt and hid them in an empty earthen jar. He left with the Mauser C96 in his waist.

He did not leave without cautioning Ge Long, "Bolt the door inside and lie on the shakedown instead of venturing out. When someone asks about me, just tell him that I went to the stable to feed the horse."

Soon after ada's departure, Ge Long could no longer lie on the shakedown with ease.

He tossed and tuned and wriggled and rolled but still find it hard to go to sleep.

With ada braving dangers alone out there, how can I lie here doing nothing?

Ge Long could not lie there anymore.

He found a window right above the shakedown. He rolled and rose on the shakedown and threw himself toward the window.

Well, I don't care if I can't go out any longer since I can look out of the window now.

Ge Long placed his face against the window pane.

Ge Long was amazed: the window may be small, but the world outside is big!

What he saw was like a well sunk in the banana grove and the Black Gem caravansary was located right at its bottom.

Through the window, he got a panoramic view of the surroundings consisting of nothing but thick banana trees encircling the seemingly small caravansary.

Fortunately, there was no lid on top of the well so that a large chunk of the sky remained.

Looking up into the sky, he saw some clouds drifting leisurely.

At the top of the banana grove where the clouds were visible, there appeared a moving black dot.

At first, Ge Long did not think much of it, treating it as a wild bird.

But, when the small black dot flew above the caravansary, it descended slowly, slowly, and, to Ge Long's astonishment, appeared to be a black kite flapping its grayish wings.

Ge Long barely gave out a cry of alarm.

Isn't it the black kite owned by Grandpa Gong Bu?

The neck raising high, the wings flipping and spreading out, and the flying posture of striking beauty—everything is so familiar! So familiar!

This is it! This is it!

The sight of the black kite moved Ge Long to tears…

Oh black kite! Black kite! Why are you here?

You've left Grandpa Gong Bu for quite some time. Why don't you go home?

Do you know how much Grandpa Gong Bu and I have been missing you? Why did you leave us in the first place?

Instead of responding to Ge Long, the black kite dived straight toward the bamboo house down below.

Ge Long's eyes followed the descending black kite closely till it landed on the roof of the bamboo house.

He saw Pu Linuo standing on the deck with a white towel in his hand. He was looking up, expecting to greet the diving black kite.

Alighting on the roof of the stilt bamboo house, the black kite fluttered its wings a bit before withdrawing them.

It must have been too tired to fly on and had to stop to rest on this bamboo house.

Ge Long thought to himself in silence. Grandpa Gong Bu said that black kites never land on strangers' bamboo houses.

But soon, an absolutely unexpected scene caught Ge Long by surprise:

The black kite waddled a few steps and went in through the skylight on the side of the bamboo house's roof the same way it got into Grandpa Gong Bu's bamboo house.

Gee! What's going on?

Ge Long blinked at this hard-to-believe phenomenon.

However, the black kite did disappear.

And it left behind the dark skylight staring like a single eye into the eyes of the stunned Ge Long.

The black kite went into the bamboo house.

So did Pu Linuo.

It's strange! The black kite is inarguably Grandpa Gong Bu's. But why did it get into the bamboo house of this caravansary?

Did it mistake this bamboo house as Grandpa Gong Bu's?

Can it be a different black kite that looks exactly like Grandpa Gong Bu's?

For a time, questions popped up in his mind like the water gurgling out of the spring under the black gemstone down below.

Ge Long had never had so many questions coming up at the same time.

Yes, they proved to be too many.

Ge Long could no longer stay in the bamboo house. He decided to go out and get to the bottom of it.

I must go and see what in the world is happening!

He removed the wood bar against the door from inside. He had just opened the door when he changed his mind...

If I go out like this, what if I run into someone from the caravansary?

He looked at the rear window. Well, if I jump out of it, I can get into the dense banana grove.

Placing the wood bar against the door again, he came to the rear window.

But he hesitated again.

This rear window faces the window of Pu Linuo's bamboo house. If I jump out here, what if Pu Linuo catches sight of me?

Ge Long was at a loss.

Scratching his head, he looked around in search of something, but he did not know what.

Suddenly, his eyes fell upon the corner where the sundries were piled up. There, he spotted a spade.

He got hold of the spade and tried it in his hand. Its pointed tip was very sharp.

That gave him an idea!

Spade in hand, Ge Long pussyfooted to the thick chestnut wood column in the middle of the bamboo house. He removed a few empty baskets piled up there to reveal the floor bamboo strips.

Slanting the spade, he chopped off some of the bamboo strips.

He soon cut a hole in the floor.

I did it! Ge Long exclaimed silently.

Ge Long backed down through the hole and reached his hand back up to conceal the opening with a basket. Holding the column with his legs, he slid down to the ground.

The floor of the stilt bamboo house surrounded by the banana trees was only half a man's height from the ground.

As soon as his feet touched the ground, Ge Long lay down on his stomach on the damp ground like a lizard perching on a wall. There, he surveyed the surroundings through the banana leaves.

It was quiet all around.

Ge Long crawled out from beneath the bamboo house and sneaked into the banana grove. Under the cover of the banana leaves, he quickly approached Pu Linuo's bamboo house and successfully maneuvered under it.

Lying on the damp dirt ground, Ge Long raised his face to look for a gap in the floor covered with a bamboo mat.

It did not take him too long to find one.

What he saw in the bamboo house through the gap shocked him...

The black kite that had flown into the bamboo house was now standing majestically on the beam.

There is no mistake about it. It is indeed Grandpa Gong Bu's black kite!

I saw Pu Linuo taking out a thumb-size bamboo tube from under the black kite's tail.

Yikes!

A bamboo tube!

Ge Long's heart thumped as if there was a rabbit jumping in his chest.

He widened his eyes and fixed them on the bamboo tube.

Pu Linuo held the bamboo tube in his hand and shook it a little. Then he gingerly pulled a roll from it and unfolded it slowly.

Ge Long saw it clearly. It was a piece of a banana leaf!

Then, a voice came from a dark corner:

"What does it the letter tell us?"

Ge Long immediately identified the voice. It was Boss Mansa's.

A banana-leaf secret letter. Ge Long's heart thumped even faster.

The bamboo floor squeaked under Pu Linuo as he was walking to the spot above Ge Long's head.

Ge Long rolled aside in a hurry to dodge and held his breath as hard as he could.

Squeak, squeak, squeak! Pu Linuo walked pass the spot.

Ge Long rolled back to peep through the gap again.

Gee! Pu Linuo took off his shoes and placed them on the spot and covered the gap.

Now, Ge Long could see nothing.

He flipped his face so that he could press his ear on the bottom of the floor.

He overheard Pu Linuo saying, "Boss, something new has happened."

"What? What's new?"

"According to the letter, the rice-transporting horse caravan has returned to Gehei Village. None of the two caravan leaders, however, did."

"What?"

"The letter also says that the youngest son of Mang Lege named Ge Long also tagged along in secret."

Ah! Ge Long's heart skipped a beat.

Isn't this referring to me?

Who delivered the letter?

Why does he know so much?

Why can he use Grandpa Gong Bu's black kite to send the message?

"The train of horses returned itself," mumbled Boss Mansa. "And a Ge Long also came out…the youngest son? It was said before that two people came out, one in black and the other in blue. Now, there's a kid too many! It's odd. Why did the caravan return? Two caravan leaders, and the kid, why didn't they return…?"

Silence reigned in the bamboo house.

Pu Linuo's lips quivered a little and said, "Neither Zhena nor Duomu have returned to us."

"You're right!" snorted Boss Mansa, "I have an idea. To kill chickens, we don't mind if they are roosters or hens. Tomorrow, we'll get our fellow fighters together and storm out of the forest under the cover of heavy fog. We'll besiege Gehei Village and do away the few armed Han Chinese so that we'll get some good weapons and ammo. Then, we'll loot the village and get enough food and clothing before we get back."

"Boss, a saying goes 'Sharpening the axe won't delay the cutting of firewood.' Good preparation saves time and lives. We can't rush. We don't have the oral message yet. The situation is still murky. If we ventured out, we might suffer." Pu Linuo gave a sigh and continued, "After we killed three of their scouts that had penetrated into the forest, the black kite's wings were injured by something or someone. For five days, we kept it in our caravansary and the channel of information was cut off at the same time. If it had not flown back this morning, we would know nothing about what is going on as if we were blind and deaf."

I see! Ge Long said to himself as the conversation he had overheard told him everything.

No wonder the black kite had left Grandpa Gong Bu for five days. That's what has happened!

It must be Ba Muli who uses Grandpa Gong Bu's black kite to send information.

Boss Mansa said, "It's so strange! Neither the caravan nor Zhena and Duomu show up. Why?"

Pu Linuo responded, "I've sent Teyue out to find out on horseback." Then he lowered his voice, "Boss, the letter mentions a father and son. The new guests that have just arrived are also a father and son."

"You mean…'

"Even a tiger sleeps with one eye open."

"Yes, that makes sense. We must be vigilant. Since we know their names, we'll surprise them. The kid is sure to betray themselves. Go and get someone to watch them!"

Oh, no! Something terrible could happen! Ge Long mumbled to himself.

What he had overheard gave him goose bumps.

I must get back to the bamboo house where we stay.

Oh, no! If I did so, they would watch us, and that would be as bad as house arrest.

I can't let them do that.

Ada is not aware of all this. I must tell him at once.

He had very little time to think, and racked his kid's brain hard.

But of all the possible solutions, there is only one option, namely to go back to the bamboo house and wait for ada there.

Fortunately, they still have no idea who we really are. I'll tackle them when problems arise.

As long as Ada learns about everything, he'll be resourceful enough to deal with them.

Ge Long made up his mind. But he had just turned around to leave when he gasped with horror:

A snake as thick as a man's wrist was staring at him with its bulging eyes in a head that was raised toward him. The snake cut off his way out from the rear!

Darn! I'm bare-handed. What shall I do?

One bite would kill me!

The snake slithered closer to Ge Long.

Holding his breath and remaining motionless, Ge Long was trying to seek an opportunity to dodge its ferocious attack.

After a moment's silent stalemate, the sight of the snake suddenly delighted Ge Long:

Its head is round instead of triangular. Its tail isn't abruptly tapered.

Ha-ha! It isn't poisonous at all!

Ge Long was now emboldened. The worst scenario was getting two bite marks, which would be no big deal.

Reaching out both his hands, he pounced upon the snake.

I'll get hold of the snake's most vulnerable part and debilitate it.

As soon as it saw Ge Long throwing his upper body upon it, the snake wriggled its body and slid away.

But the fall of Ge Long's upper body on the ground produced a slight thumping sound.

"There's a stir beneath the house!" Boss Mansa screamed.

"I'll go and take a look!"

Pu Linuo went out of the bamboo house with floor and staircase squeaking under his feet.

Like a panicky muntjac, Ge Long rolled and crawled out of spot beneath the bamboo house and hid himself behind a banana tree.

Out of the bamboo house, Pu Linuo bent over and looked beneath the house, only to see the snake slithering out.

"Well, it's a snake trying to catch a mouth."

Pu Linuo returned to the bamboo house grumbled.

It was a close call. On all fours, Ge Long crawled and scurried, crouching low, nonstop until he found himself under his bamboo house.

He looked up and found the hole was still stopped up by the basket. Everything was fine.

Ge Long held the thick column with his hands and legs, and with little effort, climbed up. He pushed aside the basket and popped his head into the hole. Grabbing the edge of the hole with both hands and pushing down hard with his elbows, he propelled his upper body into the house. He reached out a hand and was about to pull his body forward when it was hit by something that could bite...

The hand that he had reached forward was pinned under a big, cold foot.

"Ah!"

Screaming in alarm, Ge Long looked up, only to find two hairy legs propping a man as strong as a horse, with his eyes opened as wide and big as chestnuts.

Sensing trouble, Ge Long tried to get away. He was about to slide down when the man's another foot stepped on his back and pressed him down.

The foot weighed on his back like a big rock, making him hard to breathe.

Then, the man stooped down, grabbed Ge Long by his neck, and pulled him up like plucking a turnip from the soil. Ge Long cried for pain.

"See if you can cry again!"

As he finished saying so, the man gave Ge Long a punch in his stomach.

The punch caused Ge Long to gasp so that he was unable to cry out again.

Then, another punch was delivered to Ge Long's forehead.

What a ruthless punch!

It knocked poor Ge Long out of consciousness, and he lay on the floor of the bamboo house as limp as a dead lamb...

Chapter 5

Here was what happened to Mang Lege.

After parted company with Ge Long, Mang Lege sneaked out of the stilt bamboo house and into the banana grove. Through the banana leaves, he observed the layout of the caravansary and surveyed its surrounding terrain carefully.

Mang Lege found a wall of his height on the edge of the banana grove that seemed to overwhelm the caravansary. The wall was made of tree trunks tightly bound together, and the trunks were overgrown with thorns and covered with vines.

Hidden in the banana grove, it was only visible at a close range.

The wall encircling the caravansary had a main gate in the front yard and a secret small door at the backyard.

Behind the small door, there was a path leading into the dark Yuehagu Forest.

In the vicinity of the small door, part of the stable showed in the banana grove.

Mang Lege decided to take a look at the stable.

There were seven or eight horses tethered in the stable. Chestnut was on the very outside.

Perhaps the other horses did not welcome a newcomer; they stared at Chestnut with discontent while snorting at it. However, the latter was too fatigued by the long trip and focused on eating the feed while swishing its tail to shoo away the blow flies bent on stinging its rump. Sometimes, the flies tried to attack it on its belly, and it would scare them away by twitching its belly muscles.

Mang Lege went up to Chestnut and patted it on its forehead.

Chestnut recognized its master. It raised its head and rubbed its face on his shoulder.

There was not much fodder left in the trough.

Mang Lege looked around at the fodder storage room beside the stable, only to see its door ajar. He pushed it open and entered.

The fodder storage room was dark without windows. In the dim light seeping through the cracks of the bamboo-fence walls, he could see several big haystacks.

Mang Lege was reaching out to pick up a stack…

…when all of a sudden he heard a flop. It seemed that something slipped from the haystack he was carrying in his arms and dropped to the haystacks.

Mang Lege did not pay too much attention at first, thinking of it as nothing but a stone mixed in the haystack.

He glanced at it casually.

But the glance shocked him...

It was an ear that had dropped to the haystacks.

A man's ear!

Mang Lege crouched down immediately and picked up the dehydrated human ear.

It was an ear in its entirety, which meant that it had been neatly cut by a sharp knife.

Mang Lege gave a shudder, as if he could hear the blood-curdling scream of the torture victim.

The accidental discovery of a human ear alerted Mang Lege to this dark fodder storage room.

He lifted each of the haystacks and examined the columns, the walls, and the ceiling.

Before long, he discovered something new:

At the base of a column, there were some dark-brown blood stains.

They looked like some marks.

But it was too dim in the room for him to see clearly.

Mang Lege lay down on his stomach. Holding the column in one arm, he bent some of the bamboo strips on a fence wall to allow sunlight to flood in.

Now, he saw it clearly. These marks of blood stains were a line of scribbled text:

The caravansary is a lair of bandits.

The text written in blood was like fire that kindled Mang Lege's anger like hay.

He felt his whole body burning hot, as if flames were jetting out of his eyes, nose, mouth, and ears.

There was no doubt that this bloody piece of intelligence had been left by his comrade-in-arm before his death.

He may have been brutally tortured by the bandits and killed right in this dark room.

Mang Lege's eyes were blurred by the tears streaming down his cheeks.

Flashing in front of his mind's eye were the smiling faces of the three comrades-in-arm who had left never to return…

Suddenly, a horse was heard galloping closer and closer from the distance.

Mang Lege strained his ears and found the hoof-beats somehow muffled. They were barely audible if he had not listened intently.

The hoof-beats stopped somewhere close to the small door to the backyard.

Someone jumped off the horse nimbly. Then, the small door was pushed open squeaking.

After leading the horse into the backyard, the man came straight to the stable.

Mang Lege's heart jumped a beat as he found it impossible for him to get out.

He cast a quick glance around the fodder storage room, aware that he was in an extremely dangerous situation. If the man cornered him in the room, a life and death struggle would ensue. If things went wrong, they would make lots of noises that would alert the bandits nearby. Then his reconnaissance mission would be doomed.

Mang Lege pussyfooted to the door of the storage room, where he popped his head out to look about. It was quiet all around. He was about to step out when he heard footsteps thumping in the banana grove.

Mang Lege quickly backed into the fodder storage room.

Someone entered the stable.

Soon, the man who had led the horse into the backyard also came into the stable.

"Teyue, how're things going?" asked the one who had first entered the stable.

Mang Lege could tell from the voice that it was Pu Linuo.

"It's a long story. I went all the way to the Lanmang River, but couldn't run into even a ghost!"

Gee, how come this Teyue sounds so familiar? Mang Lege asked himself.

Mang Lege stole a look at him. What? It was none other than Big Opening Mouth! The "guest" with whom he had drunk wine!

Mang Lege took a closer look and found the hoofs of Teyue's horse wrapped in thick coir fibers.

No wonder the hoof-beats were so quiet!

"Not even a ghost to ran into? A pestle can never get out of a mortar no matter how high it's lifted. It looks like I was right when I asked Bang Queli to watch that father and son. Come back here when you park the horse. I'm going to tell the boss what's going on."

With that, Pu Linuo turned and left.

"Oh, darn!" Mang Lege said to himself, "Pu Linuo is keeping a close watch on me and Ge Long."

Mang Lege got anxious.

If that Bang Queli realized that Ge Long was alone in the bamboo house, things could instantly go out of hand.

What shall I do? The intelligence I've got consists of nothing but a few insubstantial clues.

The Black Gem caravansary is the lair of the bandits…

There's a mole in Gehei Village…

The mole keeps communicating with Boss Mansa…

Boss Mansa directs the actions of the bandits in the forest in accordance with the mole's intelligence…

Yet these clues are not enough to work out a plan to lure the bandits out of the forest.

But the current situation is so precarious that further investigation seemed to be impossible. If something goes awry, we can't even send out the information we've already obtained.

What shall I do then?

Mang Lege was feeling as if he were on a knife-edge when he heard footfalls thumping and thumping…

The big-opening mouth Teyue plodded toward the fodder storage room.

On the point of being cornered in the dark room at any moment, Mang Lege became bellicose.

He quickly pulled his Mauser C96 from the back of his waist.

No! If I fired, hell would break loose in the caravansary.

Mang Lege swallowed. Having changed his mind, he hid himself behind the door, ready to hit Big Opening Mouth to the floor with the grip of his gun.

But in the blink of an eye, he changed his mind again.

This won't do, either.

Pu Linuo hasn't gone far. If he heard a stir, the plan would also fall out.

I'd better find a hiding place in the room. I'll get rid of him in case he discovers me.

Having made up his mind, Mang Lege tiptoed to the end of the fodder storage room. He lay low behind the haystacks.

Squeak...

The bamboo door was pushed open.

The light behind the door cast Teyue's dark, slanting shadow on the floor.

Mang Lege holed up in the dark, fixing his eyes on the dark figure.

The silhouette of Teyue balked at the door for quite some time.

Can it be that he's discovered me? Mang Lege asked himself.

Shuffling, shuffling, shuffling...

Teyue walked on the hay covering the floor toward the haystacks shielding Mang Lege.

As the footsteps approached, Mang Lege pressed the trigger of his handgun.

Shuffling, shuffling, shuffling...

Teyue was coming closer and closer.

Mang Lege pressed the trigger harder.

Just then, Teyue stopped.

Scooping a haystack, Teyue turned around and walked out of the fodder storage room.

Shuffling, shuffling, shuffling...

He didn't see me.

As he was thinking so, Mang Lege popped his head from behind the haystacks, gazing steadily at the opened bamboo door.

From the outside of the bamboo door came the sound of Teyue adding fodder to the horse feed in the troughs.

As he was working, Teyue hummed a tune:

> A little crab has eight legs, oh!
>
> Moving sideways and to and fro,
>
> To the riverbank you move slow.
>
> Oh, once there you pinch my toe...

After he finished adding fodder, he dawdled in the stable.

Mang Lege listened carefully, assuming that he was untying the coir fibers from the horse's hoofs.

After a while, Teyue thumped out of the stable and into the banana grove, humming the same tune.

Like a muntjack venturing out to water, Mang Lege pricked his ears, listening to Teyue walking away further and further:

Brother crab, I'll subdue you,

You'd better loosen my toe…

His footfalls gradually disappeared in the depth of the banana grove.

Only then did Mang Lege straighten up his back.

Scooping a haystack, he pushed the bamboo door open intuitively, walked out of the fodder storage room, and placed the hay to the mouth of Chestnut.

After feeding the horse, Mang Lege listened about carefully but did not hear anything. He was about to walk out of the stable when he suddenly felt a gust of wind behind his head. He dodged it nimbly. A thick club came down skimming across his ear with a bang. It struck the trough dug out of a tree trunk and knocked half of it off, causing a commotion among the horses.

What a narrow escape!

But for his nimbleness, Mang Lege's skull would have been smashed.

Mang Lege shuddered at the impact with which the trough had been shattered.

Turning around, he found the sneaky striker none other than the big-opening mouthed Teyue.

It turned out that this thug had discovered Mang Lege as soon as he entered the fodder storage room. Barehanded, he pretended not to see lest he might suffer. Therefore, he took the haystack and fed the horse. He then sneaked into the banana grove, giving Mang Lege the impression that he had walked into the distance.

In reality, he had not gone anywhere. He simply stamped his feet and hummed the tune where he was.

He stamped his feet incrementally lightly and gradually faded out his humming. At the same time, he plucked a thick stick used to support a banana tree, pussyfooted around, and sneaked up behind Mang Lege.

Teyue meant to kill Mang Lege with the sudden blow but had never expected that the he would be able to dodge it.

Though it had missed Mang Lege, the strike had such an impact that it numbed striker's hands.

No longer able to hold the stick, Teyue cast it. Sticking up his neck, he bumped his head into Mang Lege.

After evading the club, Mang Lege was still out of balance. Teyue's bump in his stomach caught him off guard. He immediately felt his head swim and his breath short while his stomach was as painful as if a knife was trusted into it.

He was bumped a few steps back and almost fell to the ground.

Now that he found himself getting the upper hand, Teyue began to feel strength coming back in his numbed hands. He held them into fists and delivered a punch to each side of Mang Lege's rib case. With "whack-whack," Mang Lege felt limp and thudded to the ground on his back.

Seizing the opportunity, Teyue pounced upon Mang Lege like a tiger while reaching out to place his hands around the latter's neck.

Before Teyue's punches reached his rib case, Mang Lege suddenly straightened out his right hand and put the tips of his five fingers together to form the shape of a triangle like a chicken head. Then he unexpectedly trusted it into Teyue's big opening mouth.

Without knowing the lethality of this move, Teyue tried to close his mouth to bite the hand.

Mang Lege's five-finger "chicken head" was as tough as the tip of an iron rod. The thrust caused Teyue to feel nausea and to open his mouth as if to vomit.

Teyue had just opened his mouth when Mang Lege drove his "chicken-head" fingers deeper into his throat.

This jab tuned Teyue's insides upside down. He retched violently.

Mang Lege followed the jab up closely with another push of his right hand into Teyuc's esophagus!

This was too much for Teyue. He stopped breathing temporarily, hung his head sideways, and showed the whites of his eyes. He dropped from Mang Lege's grip to the floor thudding.

Mang Lege sprang up, pulled his hand out of Teyue's mouth, took off his waistband, slipped it around Teyue's neck, and pulled it tight until he kicked the bucket.

After getting rid of Teyue, Mang Lege heaved a deep sigh.

Wiping the sweat off his face, he covered Teyue's body with hay, sped out of the stable, and sneaked into the banana grove.

Mang Lege strode quickly through the banana grove.

He was to join Ge Long.

But when he neared his stilt bamboo guest house, he suddenly caught sight of a horrifying scene.

A dark-faced stout man was coming out of the bamboo house carrying under his arm Ge Long, who he had knocked out of consciousness.

Mang Lege saw red. He pulled out his Mauser C96, rushed out of the banana grove, and planted himself in front of the dark-faced man.

This bandit, Bang Queli by name, paused in a flurry.

They glared at each other with aggressiveness.

Coming upon each other, the two adversaries each were thinking hard of a way to crush the other.

Bang Queli suddenly pulled Ge Long to his front from under his arm where he had carried him horizontally. He used Ge Long as a human shield when threatened at Mang Lege's gun point. Then he backed to the bamboo house step by step.

Bang Queli's move was just what Mang Lege had hoped for because he had feared that a protracted exposure in the open would risk being seen by other bandits.

Bang Queli backed into the bamboo house.

Mang Lege pressed on closely.

With a roar, Bang Queli held Ge Long up as if he were a rock and threw him at Mang Lege.

Mang Lege reached out and received his son in his arms.

At this very moment, Bang Queli launched a kick and knocked the handgun off Mang Lege's hand.

While focusing on Ge Long, Mang Lege failed to anticipate the attack. He turned around quickly and placed Ge Long on the shakedown.

When he looked back, he caught sight of Bang Queli bending over to pick up the gun. He stepped forward in time and stamped on Bang Queli's hand.

The stamp hurt Bang Queli so much that he let go the gun, his face distorted by agony.

Before Bang Queli had a chance to straighten his back, Mang Lege punched him in the cheek.

Bang! Mang Lege felt as if he had hit a rock.

While Mang Lege felt his hand numb, Bang Queli seemed to be unaffected at all. Grinning and chuckling, he seemed to be in no mood to fight back.

Regardless of the consequences, Mang Lege delivered another punch in his cheek.

The punch was again landed as if on a rock. Bang Queli did not even wince his shoulder.

A fixed look assured Mang Lege that this thug, who was a head taller than he was, was puffing out both his cheeks. "I see!" Mang Lege said to himself, "This guy is well-trained in martial arts." Looking down, he saw him bulging his abdomen at the same time.

Mang Lege now realized that this bandit was practicing qigong. Mang Lege was perturbed by the fact that it was impossible to get him under control with a few punches and kicks.

Having withstood the two punches, Bang Queli began to be complacent.

Grinning hideously, he pressed toward Mang Lege swaggering.

As he stepped back, Mang Lege was trying to figure out a countermeasure. He was backing and backing when his heel hit an earthen jar. He turned around, picked it up, and started clobbering Bang Queli on his head with it.

Bang Queli turned his head aside and dodged the jar.

The jar crashed into pieces on the column of the house.

The time he tried banging Bang Queli with the jar, Mang Lege also took a sudden stride forward and landed his punch on Bang Queli's left eye. Bang Queli screamed with excruciating pain. Mixed with blood, his liquefied broken eye oozed out red and blue.

Mang Lege followed up this successful blow with another punch, aiming at his right eye.

He meant to knock Bang Queli completely blind, but the latter dodged his punch by tilting his head aside.

The momentum threw Mang Lege out of balance. Bang Queli lifted his knee abruptly and hit Mang Lege in his stomach like an iron ball. Mang Lege stooped with anguish. Taking this opportunity, Bang Queli raised his machete-like palm and let it fall hard on the back of Mang Lege's stretched neck.

This hacking palm sent Mang Lege staggering and finally collapsing to the floor.

Mang Lege knew clearly that if he fell, he would certainly suffer a fatal blow.

He quickly reached out both his hands trying to push himself up.

Bang Queli stepped forward swiftly and chopped Mang Lege hard on the back of his neck with his palm.

This blow was so devastating that Mang Lege felt as if his neck had been hit by a hand hay cutter. He plopped to the floor on all fours.

Bang Queli pounced upon his back, pressing Mang Lege's neck with one hand, and pulled a knife from the back of his waist with the other. He was thrusting it down…

…when, at this whoosh, a spade flew over at this juncture of life and death.

The sharp pointed tip of the space went straight toward Bang Queli's forehead.

Bang Queli screamed with terror, but it was too late.

The spade flew whistling with its point glinting.

Phhhfft!

Ouch!

Like an emptied sack, Bang Queli crumpled onto the floor.

The spade vibrated a bit as its tip dug in Bang Queli's forehead, and from the crescent-shaped wound, purplish blood spurted out.

The one who had dealt this deadly blow to Bang Queli with a spade was none other than Ge Long!

Mang Lege rushed over, held him in his arms, and repeated, "My good son! My good son!"

"Ada, I regained consciousness quite a while ago, but I just couldn't find the favorable opportunity to hit him."

"You did a great job!"

"Ada, as soon as you let, I went out…"

Ge Long told Mang Lege everything that he had seen and heard in one breath.

Now, everything was clear to Mang Lege.

As it turns out, Grandpa Gong Bu's black kite is the "liaison" between Gehei Village and the Black Gem caravansary.

The death of all the three scouts who entered the forest one after another has to do with this black kite.

When the black kite, injured accidentally, was unable to deliver secret letters, the mole, after learning about the bandit-suppressing troops' anticipated arrival at Gehei Village, had asked Guo Sha to tell Boss Mansa about the important information by taking his opportunity of participating in the reconnaissance mission in the forest.

But after Guo Sha set out, the convalesced black kite flew back to Gehei Village again. So, the mole immediately used it to inform Boss Mansa of a person dressed in blue going to tell him the information he needs face-to-face. The black kite, however, reached Boss Mansa ahead of Guo Sha. After receiving the intelligence, Boss Mansa sent Zhena and Duomu to meet Guo Sha on the way.

Subsequently, everything went wrong, which triggered a chain of reactions.

Now, it appeared to Mang Lege that Boss Mansa was eager to capture Gehei Village. He did not know much about the coming bandit-suppressing troops yet, and he directed the bandits' operations according to the intelligence delivered by the black kite. Mang Lege believed that this much information about the bandits could help work out a smart battle plan to lure the bandits out of the forest...

The thought galvanized Mang Lege, who said to Ge Long,

"Ge Long, we've accomplished our mission. We must leave immediately and bring the information we've obtained back."

When he finished, Mang Lege put his Mauser C96 in his waistband and took out the two stick grenades from the earthen jar.

Ge Long said, "Ada, you've got three pieces of weaponry, but I have none."

Mang Lege picked up the knife from the floor and said, "Here you go. Take this, and it may be of help."

Mang Lege took Ge Long to the stable, unleashed Chestnut, wrapped its hoofs with coir fibers, sneaked out of the small door in the backyard, and disappeared in the Yuehagu Forest.

Before long, Pu Linuo came to the bamboo house used for storage and where he had put Mang Lege and Ge Long.

Pussyfooting up the staircase, he was about to peep in through the crack of the bamboo door when it was pushed open from inside squeaking.

Bang Queli reclined against the doorframe, his bloody face in both hands. He simply looked like a three-eyed monster when he moved his hands away.

"Gosh!"

Pu Linuo was so scared that he was out of tune as he screamed.

Bang Queli opened his blood clogged mouth with a tremendous effort and muttered,

"...ran...ran away..."

Before he finished, he fell thudding on the floor, like a tree cut off from the middle.

"Ran away? Where can you run? The Yuehagu Forest is like a tiger cage or a hawk-catching net. They can never get out of it. Go after them! Track them down!" ordered Boss Mansa when he learned about the escape of Mang Lege and his son. He was so wrathful that his eyes almost popped out of their sockets. "To return to Gehei Village, they can't veer from the caravan path. Go, go after them! Kill them both, father and son! Take no prisoners! You must catch up with them. You must kill them!"

Boss Mansa's assumption was right. Mang Lege and his son were exactly following the caravan path back.

They could not deviate from it.

If they did, they would be lost in the Yuehagu Forest.

With Ge Long in Mang Lege's arms, they galloped on Chestnut's back along the caravan path.

As they galloped for a long time, the coir fibers wrapped around the horse's hoofs were worn out.

Clip-clop! Clip-clop!

The clatter of the horse's hoofs was audible again.

It reached far and wide in the quiet forest.

Overlapping echoes of the clip-clops seemed to be coming from the depth of the forest.

But, Mang Lege identified the echoes as disorderly instead of overlapping, and they were not the clip-clops of one but a team of horses.

That was too bad! The bandits were coming!

Mang Lege applied some pressure on Chestnut's belly with both legs, and the horse sped like mad.

"Ada, what's going on?"

"They're catching up."

"Can our horse outpace theirs?"

"What if it can't?"

"Then we'll stop to beat them up?"

"What if we can't beat them?"

"Can't beat them? Why can't we?"

"They outnumber us."

"…then we'll fight till we die!"

"No we can't do that, Ge Long. Remember, our mission is to send our intelligence back. We must send it back no matter what!"

"Then, I'll do whatever you tell me to!"

At that moment, the clip-clops became increasingly louder.

Looking back, Mang Lege could see the bandit charging in front of the team.

He pulled his Mauser C96 and cocked the hammer.

Just then, bang, bang! The bandits fired first.

The bullets skimmed whistling across the top of their heads and rustled the trees when they hit them.

"Son of a gun! They fired the first shot. You'll see who's a sharper shooter!"

Mang Lege pointed his Mauser C96 backwards and fired…

Bang! Bang!

The two bandits running ahead fell off their horses to bit the dust.

But the bandits behind them charged over and fired more shots.

Mang Lege fired another couple of shots and killed one more bandit.

Suddenly, he felt his right calf was struck as if it were stung by a scorpion.

Darn! I was hit! Mang Lege was thinking.

"Ge Long, we can't run on horseback anymore. Their gunshots are too dense and close!"

"What shall we do then?"

"Do as I tell you. Get ready to get off the horse!"

As he said so, Mang Lege applied some pressure on the horse's belly again, which caused serious pain to his calf though.

Chestnut seemed to understand what its master meant. Pricking up its ears, it galloped like wind, as if it were flying, leaving the pursuing bandits far behind.

Seeing that the bandits out of sight, Mang Lege pulled up on the reins and stopped the horse by an Indian-almond tree.

Chestnut reared neighing and halted.

This gave Mang Lege a favorable chance to roll off the horse carrying Ge Long under his arms.

When his right leg touched the ground, he jerked back a little with pain.

His move caught Ge Long's notice, and he asked,

"Ada, your leg is bleeding!"

Fresh blood oozed from the leg of his pants and dripped to the grassy ground.

"Nothing to be afraid of. It just scraped my skin. Hurry, get into the forest."

"What about the horse?"

"We'll let him run for us for a while."

As he said so, Mang Lege patted Chestnut on its sweating neck with grief.

Chestnut turned his head and leaned it closely against Mang Lege.

Ge Long found this chestnut horse that had carried him out of Gehei Village shedding tears in silence.

Ah, it's crying because it knows that we're going to part company.

A poor thing!

Mang Lege let go the reins and said to Chestnut:

"Go, buddy. We'll never forget you!"

As soon as he finished, he gave it a punch on its buttocks.

Chestnut turned head to take a look at Mang Lege and Ge Long as a gesture of farewell. Then, it raised its head and galloped away, clip-clop, clip-clop, along the caravan path into the depth of the forest.

Taking Ge Long by the hand, Mang Lege led him into the forest across the grassy land.

Before long, the bandits traced Chestnut's clip-clops to the Indian-almond tree and galloped pass it on their pursuit.

Pu Linuo who brought the rear of the bandits seemed to find something wrong with his small and yet sharp eyes. Suddenly, he stopped his horse by pulling up on the reins, and screamed to the bandits charging ahead,

"Stop! Stop"

The bandits paused in a flurry, looking at each other puzzled.

Pointing at the base of the Indian-almond tree, Pu Linuo shouted,

"Blood!"

Chapter 6

Blood oozed nonstop from the wound to his calf.

Holding back his pain, Mang Lege staggered on in the pathless forest, a stick in one hand as a cane to support himself and the Mauser C96 in the other.

Ge Long was hewing a path in the front with the trailing-pointed knife, cutting off the vines blocking their way.

The further they proceeded, the darker the forest became.

The dimly blue phosphorescent light flickered up from the dead wood of broken trees and the remains of dead animals in the depth of the forest.

The father and son were plodding ahead when all of a sudden, a man with a gun in hand darted from behind an Indian-almond tree.

His features were indistinctive in the dim light, only the whites of his eyes could be seen ablaze with menace below a black-cloth headwear.

"Stop!"

The man shouted while pointing his gun at Mang Lege.

A threat out of the blue stunned Mang Lege.

While Mang Lege was still dazed, the man pressed his forefinger on the trigger and pulled.

He wanted to kill Mang Lege before the latter got the upper hand of him.

Hitting upon an idea in desperation, Mang Lege raised his stick and swiped it hard…

Bang!

The bullet flew into the sky.

Before the guy had a chance to fire the second shot, Mang Lege leveled his Mauser. Bang!

Ouch…

The bullet went straight through the man's chest.

But the two gunshots attracted a hubbub of shouts.

"Over there!"

"Go and close in on them!"

"Hurry! Hurry!"

Footfalls soon followed the uproar.

The bandits came close again.

Mang Lege grabbed Ge Long by his shoulder and, widening his bloodshot eyes, said to him,

"Ge Long, the bandits are on hot pursuit. I'll hold them back a little here. You go first!"

"No, Ada," responded Ge Long, holding Mang Lege by his arm. "I can't go! I can't leave you here!"

"No, you can't stay! Son, we must send the information back!"

As he said so, Mang Lege produced the bamboo tube found in Guo Sha's pocket and pressed it in the hands of Ge Long, saying,

"Ge Long, you're small in stature and nimble. You must do everything you can to deliver this bamboo tube to Uncle Gu Ming. Tell him that Boss Mansa is still unaware that we've discovered the secret of the black kite. Neither is he aware that the bandit-suppressing troops will arrive in Gehei Village soon. He's anxious to besiege the village. We can use the black kite to lure the bandits out of the Yuehagu Forest and wipe them out!"

Now, the bandits were drawing closer and closer.

Mang Lege said in a haste,

"Go now, Ge Long! When you lose your bearings, climb up a tall tree and look for Mount Nuocha. Do you remember?

"Yes, I do. But Ada, you…"

"Go and hurry! Don't' worry about me!"

"Ada…"

Ge Long could not hold back his tears from, which gushed from his eyes.

Seeing his son crying, Mang Lege was heartbroken.

But there was no time to linger longer.

Giving Ge Long a forceful push, he urged,

"Stop crying, Go!"

Racing a few steps, Ge Long looked back at his Ada again.

He saw Ada yanking a handgun from the hand of a fallen bandit and rushed to behind a sea bilberry tree for cover.

Then, ada also looked back.

His eyes were searching for his son as his son's eyes were following him.

Suddenly the eyes of the father and son met.

At a moment when emotional tie of a father and son was needed the most, they had to part company.

How much they wanted to say to each other, but they had to bury it in their hearts. How many tears they could have shed, but they had to swallow them back.

They gazed at each other briefly and said farewell in silence.

They left both the grief of their separation and the worries and concerns about each other to the Yuehagu Forest.

The son took away his father's look of warmth; the father kept the crystal transparency of son's eyes.

Gunshots rang out.

The bandits rushed over screaming.

Mang Lege concluded that the bandits had not located where exactly he was. He held a handgun in each hand firmly and pressed himself against the sea bilberry motionless.

The bandits had advanced as close as five or six steps away from the sea bilberry tree when Mang Lege suddenly popped out and fired with both guns. Bang! Bang! Two bandits thumped to the ground.

The other bandits all threw themselves to the ground and fired back randomly.

Gunshots surrounded the sea bilberry tree in three directions.

Short of ammunition, Mang Lege knew that he could not fire back without restraint. Therefore, he hid behind the tree, letting the bandits fire at will.

After a random shooting rampage, the bandits found that Mang Lege had not been firing back.

Pu Linuo screamed in a high pitch,

"Surround him and attack!"

The seven bandits divided themselves into three groups. One remained where they were to block Mang Lege from the front. The other two began to outflank Mang Lege from both sides under the cover of the dense trees.

Attacked from three sides, Mang Lege had to fire back.

While suppressing the bandits on the left flank with gunfire, he turned around to keep an eye on the bandits coming from the right flank.

When they figured out that Mang Lege only fired at their fellow bandits on the left flank, the two bandits on the right were emboldened. They shot their way toward Mang Lege as they sped up their advance.

Mang Lege aimed at a bandit on the right and pulled the trigger. Bang! The bandit gave a blood-curdling scream and dropped down holding his stomach with his hands. The one following him was so frightened that he rushed behind of a tree and dared not pop out his head anymore.

Just then, the bandits on the left flank came up.

Mang Lege raised his gun and fired. Clank!

The gun failed to go off.

The chamber was empty.

After firing the other gun for a while, it also went silent.

"He's run out of ammo!"

"Hurry and charge. Don't let him run away!"

"Skin him!"

Hearing that Mang Lege had run out of ammunition, the bandits appeared from behind the trees shouting blusteringly to boost their courage and began to close in on Mang Lege.

Casting the handguns, he pulled a stick grenade from his waist, unscrew the safety cap, and pulled out the cord attached to the friction igniter.

For the bandits, the temporary silence behind the Indian-almond tree was more terrifying than gunshots.

Seeing them gathering together, Mang Lege threw the stick grenade into the crowd.

Boom! Two bandits collapsed.

The only weaponry left was the one stick grenade.

The last one!

Breathing heavily, he pulled it out from his waist, unscrew the safety cap, and pulled out the cord.

If I don't kill them, they'll kill me!

And they'll run after Ge Long!

No, I can't let go none of them! None!

I'll kill them off. I can't afford to let a single one survive!

As he was thinking so, Mang Lege cast a look at the direction where Ge Long disappeared.

Ge Long, my good son, it's all up to you!

Fixing the end of the cord to his waistband and insert the grenade in it, he stood under the Indian-almond tree holding his arms in front of his chest.

One of his hand was holding the wood stick of the grenade in secret.

Before long, shuffling footsteps could be head from behind the tree.

The bandits were sneaking up.

Shuffling, shuffling, shuffling…

The footsteps were closer and closer.

All of a sudden, Pu Linuo screamed loudly,

"Charge…"

Four bandits suddenly appeared in front of Mang Lege, each holding a trailing-pointed knife in his hand.

"Well, you're a bird in the cage and a fish in the net. I'll see where you can escape?" Pu Linuo said with venom.

Mang Lege rolled his eyes in return.

Pu Linuo cast a sinister glance around and asked,

"Where's your son?"

Mang Lege forced a scornful chuckle.

"He's run away," said Pu Linuo pointing at the smaller footprints. "There's no way he'll get out alive. The Yuehagu Forest is our domain."

The other bandits echoed with uproars.

"Come over if you dare!" said Mang Lege glaring at the saber-rattling bandits.

"So what! Here we come!" At Pu Linuo's orders, the bandits pounced on Mang Lege with their knives.

Mang Lege pulled the stick grenade from his waistband with force, and, the cord hooked up to the friction igniter was detached.

Smoke spewed from the stick of the grenade.

"Good Heavens!" The terrified bandits screamed and turned to run.

Mang Lege took a stride further, kicked one of the bandits to the ground, grabbed Pu Linuo by his collar, and roared,

"No one can run away!"

His roar stunned the other two bandits so much that they stopped as if their feet were planted on the ground.

The grenade was sizzling and smoking…

But when the smoke fizzled out, the grenade did not explode!

It was a dud!

"Darn!" Mang Lege subconsciously gave out an explanation of alarm.

He raised the grenade high and whacked Pu Linuo on his head.

Pu Linuo tilted his head and dodged it.

Mang Lege missed his target, and four sharp knives were thrusted into his chest at once…

Like a fish in a huge net, Ge Long ran like mad in the Yuehagu Forest.

He lost his bearings.

He did not know which way to go.

He just kept running and running.

He ran and ran when he found the trees less dense.

Ah, have I run to the edge of the forest? He asked himself.

No, this was not the edge of the forest. It was a marsh.

Marshes are formed of constantly gushing spring water that has macerated trees and mixed them in the bog, which is then overgrown with low-lying wetland plants.

There were marshes of various sizes in the Yuehagu Forest. They were of different depth due to their formation in different times. The shallow ones were only knee-deep while the deep ones could be chest-deep or even above a man's head.

Ge Long's advance was blocked by the marsh.

At first look, it did not appear too deep.

A dozen steps in front of him was a grove of bushes connecting to the forest.

I'm small in stature and therefore light in weight. Wading across the marsh, I can dart into the forest on the other side.

It's only a dozen steps away!

He made up his mind and was about to put his foot in the marsh when a mallard fluttered out of the forest, flew across the marsh, and alighted by the side of the bushes. Before it had time to get into the bushes when suddenly, splash, a muddy crocodile emerged from the bog. Without giving the mallard a chance to fly away, the crocodile got hold of its wings in its mouth. It then crawled back wiggling its lengthy body and submerged in the march.

Ge Long gasped with horror, considering himself lucky not to have put his feet in the marsh.

The presence of such a big crocodile indicated that great depth of the bog, which could prove fatal if Ge Long had stepped into it.

Just then, a hubbub of footfalls came from the ancient forest.

The bandits were coming!

Looking around, he saw his small footprints in the mud.

These footprints were like a series of shallow pits left by a stick.

The bandits traced his footprints to him!

What am I going to do? He asked himself. He looked around, only to spot a big, slanting tree not far from him.

It's a ready-made bridge, isn't it?

Yes, I'll cross to the other side on the big tree.

He paused right before he leaped onto the big tree. On second thought, he gave the plan up, concluding that the bandits would look for his footprints here and there if they found them disappear abruptly at the marsh. Then they would figure out that he had crossed the marsh on the tree.

Now, I know what to do!

Yes, an idea dawned upon him.

He picked up a clog and cast it into the marsh. The clog slowly submerged leaving a small dent on the surface. Great! It was a success!

Ge Long threw a series of clogs into the mire, each further than the previous one until the last one went into the bush grove. The clogs gradually submerged and leaving on the surface of the marsh a conspicuous trail of dents. They looked like a series of footprints if not examined carefully.

After the feat, Ge Long hopped to the slanting tree and ran along it to the other side and into the forest.

As soon as his small figure was enveloped by the forest, Pu Linuo and his fellow bandits arrived at the edge of the marsh following his footprints.

Leading the pack was a tall, dumb-looking bandit. He caught sight of the dents on the marsh and concluded that they were Ge Long's footprints.

"He ran across the mash from here!"

The dumb-looking tall bandit rushed into the marsh yelling.

"Don't cross it!" shouted Pu Linuo who was bringing the rear.

But it was too late.

The dumb-looking tall bandit had been in the marsh, where he plodded a few steps before being bogged down.

"Oh, gosh! Oh, gosh!"

As he screamed wildly, he struggled hard with his hands waving in the air, but the harder he struggled, the deeper he sank.

The gurgling bog had swallowed half of his body.

"Help! Help!"

As if in answer to his call for help, five or six crocodiles emerged from the bush grove one after another, baring sharp teeth in their wide-open mouths. Vying with one another, they crawled into the marsh.

"Oh my gosh!" The bogged dumb-looking tall bandit let out a volley of horrifying screams punctuated with piteous pleas; "Gosh, my gosh! Pu Linuo, pull me out! Pull me out, please!"

Pu Linuo said shrugging, "I'm sorry but my arm is not long enough."

With that, he raised his gun and fired. Bang! The dumb-looking tall bandit's head was covered in blood all over.

The bog was dyed red.

Startled by the gunshot, the crocodiles submerged in the marsh immediately, showing only their dark, sparkling eyes above the surface, gazing greedily at the blood-red muddy water.

Sharp-eyed Pu Linuo soon found some of the moss on the slanting tree was rubbed off by someone running on it.

"He ran across on the tree. Go after him!"

Leading the two remaining bandits, Pu Linuo crossed the marsh along the slanting tree and continued their pursuit.

Ge Long scuttled and scuttled in the forest until he reached a huge banyan tree.

The tree reached out two boughs like a giant's arms, one pointing to the left path and the other to the right.

Ge Long hesitated a little and decided to turn to the left path. He had not run for a few steps when he paused. He cast his scabbard to the right path and resumed his scamper along the left path.

Pu Linuo came to the big banyan tree and found the paths forked into left and right. He was confused about which to follow.

He looked about and discovered the scabbard on the right path.

"Great! He's running this way!"

Pu Linuo led his two fellow bandits to the right path and resumed their pursuit.

One of his fellow bandits was named Bang Tie and the other Mang Lu.

After taking a few steps, the cunning Pu Linuo stopped to order Bang Tie, "You don't have to follow us. You go after him along the left path. Kill him when you catch up!"

Bang Tie said "yes" and changed his direction.

Taking Mang Lu with him, Pu Linuo continued with their manhunt.

After chasing for a while, he found something wrong: there were no footprints on the ground, and no movement was heard.

Blinking his eyes, he concluded that Ge Long was running along the left path. He and Mang Lu turned around and switched to it.

By this time, Bang Tie had almost caught up with Ge Long.

Ge Long ran and ran when he was stumbled over entangling vines and fell to the ground.

He picked himself up, but before he got to running again, he found Bang Tie approaching.

Bang! Bang! Bang Tie fired two shots. The bullets skimmed whistling across Ge Long's red-cloth headwear.

He threw himself to the ground in a great rush.

After the gunshots, he looked back. "Oh, my! I'm a dead meat!"

The bandit was only less than a dozen steps away from him. If he continued to run, he would be shot and killed for sure.

Ge Long spotted a grove of bushes beside him and dashed into it without delay.

While separating the branches ahead with his hands, he crawled and scampered like a tunneling bamboo rat.

Bang Tie came to where Ge Long had disappeared. The swaying bushes told him that Ge Long had sneaked into the grove. Bang Tie followed into it after he leveled his gun and fired another shot into it.

Ge Long scurried and scurried in the bushes when suddenly he caught sight of two big, black eyes gleaming in the front.

Gee! Ge Long stopped. He took a closer look, only to see a huge wild buffalo.

The wild buffalo, covered with bristling black hair, had a pair of horns with their tips as sharp as knives. Arching its back while raising its shoulders, it kept snorting and digging the muddy ground with its front hoof, assuming a fighting posture.

Needless to say, it was startled by the gunshots just fired.

At this very moment, it was so ferocious that even a tiger would be no match for it.

Ge Long had not gazed at the startled, road-blocking buffalo for a minute before the footsteps were getting closer and closer behind him.

Too bad! I'm under a pincer attack: a big-horned mad buffalo in the front and a gun-brandishing bandit from the back. What shall I do?

If I charge forward, the mad buffalo would not make way. If I battle with the bandit, it would be impossible because my life would come to an end if he should pull the trigger with his forefinger. And it was also too late to find a hideout.

I don't mind losing my life. But it would be impossible to send the information out.

Ge Long scratched his head beneath the red-cloth headwear.

His father's words instantly rang in his ears:

"A startled buffalo can't bear to see the color red."

Excitement immediately surged within him.

He sprang up and charged toward the startled buffalo unfurling his red-cloth headwear.

"Moo…"

Seeing red, the buffalo let out a mighty roar and, slanting his horns, pounced on Ge Long.

Seeing the mad buffalo dashing over, Ge Long slung the unfurled red-cloth headwear backward and, meanwhile, rolled into the bushes nearby, successfully evading the danger.

The wrathful buffalo thrusted its horns toward the red cloth and plunged itself right before Bang Tie.

Having no time to dodge, Bang Tie leveled his gun and fired.

Living in the forest, wild buffalos usually swallow in mud when it is hot and rub against trees whey they feel itchy. Therefore, they are always covered with a thick layer of dry mud and resin, as tough as iron plates. Bang Tie's shot hit its back, but the bullet just slipped away, leaving no mark at all.

The buffalo was further enraged!

Tilting its neck and bulging its eyes, it was certain that Mang Tie was its target.

Unable to stave off the buffalo's onslaught, Bang Tie fired a few random shots and took to his feet.

Bent on getting at him, the buffalo sprang to run after its target.

How could Bang Tie's two legs outpace the buffalo's four hoofs?

Soon, the buffalo cornered Bang Tie against a big-leaf tree.

Bang Tie was out of breath. He fired a shot back at the buffalo again.

His blind shot got hold of the wild buffalo's ear by a fluke. Blood dyed the ear's side of the buffalo's face red. It was so painful that it summoned all its strength, leapt up mooing aloud, and aimed its horns at the back of Bang Tie.

It was impossible for Bang Tie to dodge. With a heart-breaking shriek, he was pinned to the tree by the buffalo's horns.

Without giving up its attack, the buffalo followed up with a fierce thrust, pushing its horns squishing into Bang Tie's back.

Bang Tie limped instantly and was stuck on the tree like a piece of mud.

The buffalo quit attacking its opponent when seeing it immobile.

But it did not leave. It stood where it was in all majesty.

When Pu Linuo and Mang Lu traced the gunshots to the spot, they ran across the bloody-faced buffalo!

The two bandits were too frightened to scream. They turned and took to their heels, lest the buffalo would take their lives.

While fleeing, Pu Linuo blamed Bang Tie on his folly of fighting a wild buffalo.

Blinking his eyes, Mang Lu speculated, "Maybe the little rascal has cast a spell."

"What spell?" snorted Pu Linuo, "Even if he had wings or turned himself into a fairy, he would not be able to get out of my hand. Let's go around and chase."

By then, Gulong had covered a long distance.

He ran and ran when he found the terrain changing and all of a sudden a ravine lay before him, blocking his way.

Ge Long brought himself to a sudden halt and looked down, only to find the ravine more than forty to fifty meters deep, with a precipitous cliff rising on either side and the vaguely visible floor covered with rocks of varying sides. Running zigzag through the rocks was an extremely narrow stream. Perhaps, when flash floods broke out, this was a place where unchecked torrents would roar. But at this moment, the deep and partly dark floor of the ravine was so quiet that the chirps of the insects hiding in the cracks of the rocks were audible. The ravine was not too wide, and on the other side was a hill overgrown with trees and cogon grass. A wild sweet-scented osmanthus tree struck down by thunder lay horizontally across ravine forming a foot bridge.

Ge Long stepped on the sweet-osmanthus bridge and headed for the hill on the other side.

The sweet-osmanthus bridge had weathered so much that its outer and inner barks were already rotten and covered with slippery moss. Ge Long extended his arms to balance himself and picked his steps carefully. He had just walked a few steps when he suddenly heard footsteps coming from behind, and the bandits caught up again! At this moment, Ge Long realized that although the hill on the opposite side was overgrown with trees and grass, they were not thick, and the dim afterlight escaped between the trees.

What! It was not a forest but a cliff!

Ge Long balked on the sweet osmanthus bridge. For a moment, he was at a loss what to do between the cliff in the front and the bandits behind. Moving forward, and it was a dead end, but backing off, and he had to face the beastly bandits.

What to do?

Ge Long was so anxious that he opened his bloodshot eyes wide, looking around for a way out.

Just then, he heard the footsteps drawing closer.

With his escape route cut off, Ge Long made a desperate decision: he dashed across the sweet osmanthus bridge and hid himself in the grass on the edge of the cliff.

It was a patch of cogon grass as tall as a man's height. The serrated little prickles on the blades left multiple bloody cuts on Ge Long's hands and face. Despite all of this, he rolled and crawled into the depth of the cogon grass. He was crawling when he found a big stubby tree with a dark hole in it concealed by the tall, dense cogon grass.

He gazed at the tree hole with his wide-open eyes.

Just then, he heard Pu Linuo's shout coming from the other side of the valley,

"Alright, there're footprints on the sweet osmanthus tree!"

Mang Lu screamed as well, "This time, he has nowhere to run away!"

"Let's go! Let's cross over quickly!"

Pu Linuo and Mang Lu crossed the sweet osmanthus bridge.

It's too bad. If I go on like this, I'll ruffle the grass, and they'll discover me.

No, I can't move on any more.

I'd better hide in the tree hole.

Ge Long made up his mind. Holding the bamboo tube in his mouth, he lay close to the ground like a lizard on a wall and crawled toward the tree hole.

Finally, he crawled to the entrance of the hole. He had just pulled his upper body into it when a terrifying sight made his hair stand on end…

There was a scull-like face in the horrifying dark hole.

Before Ge Long had time to retract his upper body, a pair of big hairy hands stretched out of the hole toward his face.

At that very moment, Ge Long had a clear view: it was a black snub-nosed monkey.

The monkey did not give Ge Long the time to dodge before it scratched his face. Despite the excruciating pain that made him tremble all over, he had to be stoically quiet.

He turned sideways, and the black snub-nosed monkey dashed out of the tree hole.

And it just bumped into Mang Lu.

Mang Lu did not catch a clear view of what it was. As he turned around and ran, he screamed "Ghost! Ghost!"

Not knowing what was happening, Pu Linuo followed Mang Lu blindly.

In fact, the black snub-nosed monkey was more frightened. Seeing the two running off, it slid away from the edge of the cliff.

Running a few steps, Pu Linuo stopped and turned around, saying, "No, we can't run away. This child has vital information to send out."

Mang Lu responded, "This is such as small place. He has nowhere to run away. Let's set the grass on fire and burn him to death!"

"Right, we'll burn him to death." With that, Pu Linuo set fire to the cogon grass.

Smoke rose from the cliff as the grass was burning.

The mountain wind flared it up so abruptly that a flame almost scorched Pu Linuo's hair.

Pu Linuo said, "Let's go, otherwise it would be too late."

Before they left, the two bandits fired a few shots into the burning grass randomly.

The fire on the cliff dwindled.

As the cogon grass was burned up, the fire ran out of steam.

The damp tree hole protected Gulong.

Gulong was out of harm's way!

He crawled out of the tree hole and spat out the bamboo tube from his mouth.

Suddenly, he saw with his mind's eye the strapping figure of ada and his face filled with love.

Ada, where are you now? Where can I find you?

Ge Long looked up and around. It was as quiet as dark.

Who could answer the question?

The monkeys panic-stricken by the gunshots had by now collected themselves and sneaked out quietly. Scratching themselves and blinking their eyes, they stared dully at this lonely child.

Wind sprang up in the forest.

Ge Long shuddered in the wind.

The forest teems with beasts of prey. It's getting dark. What shall I do, Ge Long asked himself. How shall I send the intelligence out?

Ge Long remembered the tip that ada had told him of finding a way out of the forest.

He faced up, trying to find a tall tree from which he could see Mount Nuocha.

The monkeys in the trees thought that he was up to something against them. Therefore, in answer to the monkey leader's warning of danger, the whole tribe of monkeys broke up in a hubbub and fled in all directions.

As the trees were so close to one another, they hopped from one to another and vanished in the blink of an eye.

The escape of the monkeys gave Ge Long an inspiration.

I can also become a monkey and climb up to a tree and then go from one tree to another.

Then, I can not only tell where Mount Nuocha is but also keep away from the bandits and beasts of prey.

Ge Long was excited.

He climbed up to a tree nimbly.

Steadying himself on the top of this tall tree, he vaguely saw Mount Nuocha.

Wow! How beautiful Mount Nuocha was against the blue sky in the gradually advancing twilight. This was the first time Ge Long caught sight of its beauty.

While Ge Long moved toward Mount Nuocha, jumping from tree to tree like a monkey, a black kite was also flying in the same direction above his head.

This was Grandpa Gong Bu's black kite.

Carrying Boss Mansa's secret letter, it was making its last trip.

In the secret letter, it was written, "We've taken out both the father and the son."

Chapter 7

Holding its head up, the black kite stood on the rattan round table. It fixed its sparkling eyes on every move of the person.

In the dim light of dawn filtering through the rear window, a wizened hand was carving a few scribbly words on a bamboo leaf with a knife:

A heavy rain is coming.

Be sure not to go out.

Ba

The inscriber raised his head and saw through the window one or two stars still lingering on the morning sky. He tilted his head and listened around. He heard nothing stirring.

He skillfully rolled up the bamboo leaf and stuffed it gingerly into a bamboo tube.

Suddenly...

Bang!

The bamboo door was pushed open. Gu Ming and two soldiers stormed in.

The inscriber was astonished.

But he then forced a big, beaming smile as he turned around.

"He-he, good morning, Company Leader Gu Ming!"

Gu Ming responded nodding, "Not as early as you are, Grandpa Gong Bu! What information are you sending to Boss Mansa again?"

Gong Bu's face suddenly became ghastly. He hurriedly took the bamboo leaf from the bamboo tube.

Gu Ming took a quick step forward trying to seize it.

But it was too late.

Gong Bu had already rammed the bamboo leaf into his mouth and chewed it to pieces.

Gu Ming chuckled coldly and said, "We don't have to read it. I saw it clearly: you ate a bamboo leaf. That's enough evidence. According to the convention of the communication between you and Boss Mansa, you're going to send a secret letter of a bamboo leaf instead of a banana leaf."

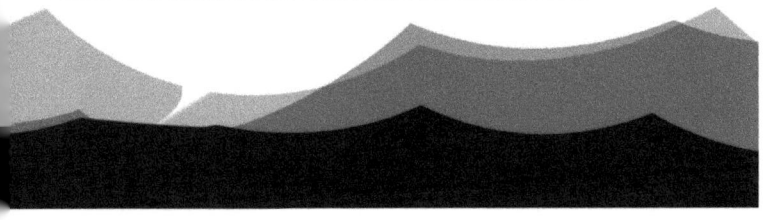

There was a murderous gleam in Gong Bu's eyes. Suddenly, he raised his sharp knife and threw himself on the black kite.

Bang!

Gu Ming's gun rang.

The bullet hit Gong Bu's hand.

Clank! The knife dropped.

Startled, the black kite fluttered into the air and alighted on the sill of the rear window, where it flickered and turned its head to look at what was going on in the stilt bamboo house.

Gong Bu stumped on the floor and shouted at the top of his lungs,

"Fly away! Fly away!"

The black kite turned its head back, flapped its wings, and darted out of the window.

Watching the black kite flying away, Gong Bu gave a snort of contempt as he put on a triumphant expression. Covering the bleeding hand with the other, he sat down on the round rattan stool.

Scrunching one of his eyebrows a bit, Gu Ming said, "Don't be happy too soon. Each time the black kite flies in the air, it circles three times above your bamboo house until you give it a signal."

As he said so, Gu Ming strode to the deck.

And he saw the black kite circling above the stilt bamboo house.

Producing a snow-white towel from his bosom, he waved it a few times above his head.

The black kite spiraled down slowly toward the bamboo house.

Gu Ming then turned to Gong Gu, saying, "If a red towel is waved, the black kite will fly to the caravansary. If you don't give any signal, it will circle three times and fly away to look for food. Sometimes, it brings some game to you in that case, am I right?"

Gong Gu shut his eyes slowly, as if he did not hear anything.

"What more plans are you devising?" Gu Ming sneered, "It's true that you have had many plans. You settled down in Gehei Village in the guise of a wanderer. You've fooled quite a few kind villagers. But you never expected that Ba Muli saw through you and Guo Sha. Unfortunately, he didn't have the guts to tell us. But it isn't too late for him to tell us now."

Just then, Ba Muli, with a black blanket draping over his shoulders, tottered to Gong Bu's bamboo house.

He staggered up to the deck and held out an arm toward the descending black kite.

The black kite, very familiar with Ba Muli, alighted on his arm steadily.

Gu Ming nodded his thanks to Ba Muli and turned to Gong Bu, saying,

"See, your black kite came back again. Sorry but we have to borrow it for a while. Boss Mansa is eager to attack Gehei Village, right? Fine! I'll have him tell all the bandits in the forest to come out of it at daybreak tomorrow. What shall we do on our part? As you know, the main force of our bandit-suppressing troops arrived here at noon today ahead of time. At midnight tonight, we'll set an ambush by the Lanmang River. Tomorrow morning, your fellow bandits will never be able to return to the Yuehagu Forest after they cross the river."

Gong Bu cast a sidelong glare at Gu Ming, his blood-shot eyes ablaze with malice, "Well, if the handwriting is different, Boss Mansa won't believe it."

"It's a shame that you have taught us how to write as you do."

With that, Gu Ming produced a piece of banana leaf and showed it to Gong Bu.

It was exactly the letter that Gong Bu had let Guo Sha delivery to the bandits.

Gong Bu let out a sigh of despondency and closed his eyes listlessly.

Suddenly, he picked up the sharp knife from the floor and pressed its blade vehemently into his own wrist.

Blood instantly squirted out from his wrist and sprayed onto the bamboo wall.

Thump! Gong Bu collapsed.

His face was as white as limestone.

The black kite took off again.

Standing on the deck, Gu Ming waved a red headwear to instruct the black kite where to fly.

The black kite flew to the Yuehagu Forest flapping its grayish wings.

Ge Long popped his head out of the window of a stilt bamboo house.

He waved to the black kite flying into the distance and shouted,

"Fly, Black Kite. This is your last flight to deliver a letter to the caravansary!"

First written in Beijing, April 8, 1982

Revised on April 18, 2018